I0678732

Surrendering to You

Sharon C. Cooper

Amaris Publishing LLC

Surrendering to You

By
Sharon C. Cooper

Copyright © 2025 Sharon C. Cooper
Amaris Publishing LLC

All rights reserved. No part of this book may be used, scanned, reproduced, uploaded, or distributed in any manner without written permission except in the case of brief quotations embodied in reviews. For permission, contact the author at https://sharoncooper.net

ISBN: 978-1-946172-63-1
Paperback

This story is a work of fiction. Names, characters, and incidents are either products of the author's imagination or are used fictitiously. Any resemblance to actual events, locales, organizations or persons, living or dead, is entirely coincidental.

Chapter One

Coffee. I need coffee.

Cree Priestly could almost taste the strong black coffee, with a shot of mocha, that she'd been craving all morning. It would be just the boost she needed to get through the second half of her busy day.

She glanced at the diamond-studded watch on her wrist, confirming she was on time as she reached the coffee shop. The short walk from her law office in downtown Chicago gave her a chance to clear her mind after a mentally exhausting morning of meetings.

As an entertainment lawyer, doing everything from reading through contracts, negotiating deals for her clients, and even helping with securing financing for film projects, there was never a dull moment. And if she was honest with herself, she loved her job and the busyness that came with it. She only wished she could say the same about the firm she worked for.

"Don't go there," she mumbled under her breath, trying to stop her mind from going down that route.

Even if things were a little tense between her and Warren

1

Ellis, one of the partners who started the firm over thirty years ago, Cree wouldn't let him derail her goals. As one of the newest managing partners, she was bringing in more clients and clocking more billable hours than any of the partners. Especially him, and he didn't like it. Sure, he liked the way their bottom line looked, but not the way she was outshining him.

Cree slowed in front of the coffee shop's large picture window, noting the wind had blown a few strands of her hair around. She quickly finger combed her short bob and, once satisfied, reached for the door handle. But before she could grab it, the door swung open.

She gasped, jumped back, and would've gotten slammed in the face if not for her quick reflexes.

"Whoa. Sorry, sweetheart. I didn't realize my own strength," the tall, light-skinned brother with pretty hazel-green eyes said as he boldly gave her a once over. "But allow me to hold the door for you, Queen. I have to say, you're the most stunning woman I've seen all day."

Cree shook her head and chuckled when the man opened the door wider, bent at the waist, and gave a slow sweeping motion with his arm for her to enter the building.

"Thank you," she mumbled, but ignored him when he asked to take her to lunch. Used to being hit on, she tuned out whatever else he was saying and went about surveying the inside of the establishment.

Besides, she was taking a break from men. It hadn't started out that way, but for the last few months, thanks to clocking in an obscene number of hours at work, she didn't have time to date. Surprisingly enough, she didn't miss the tedious task. Yes, her day job brought her in contact with some incredible men, but since she didn't date clients, their good looks and fat bank accounts were wasted on her.

When she glanced around and didn't see her sister, Essence, Cree went to the counter and ordered for them both. Usually, whoever arrived first did that, and it was always easy since they typically ordered the same thing—large black coffee and a pastry.

Five minutes later, one of the servers called out, "Priestly," and set the order on the counter before working on the next order.

Cree stepped forward, adjusting her large handbag on her shoulder, then grabbed the drink carrier and white bag that held their pastries. The place was busy, and she still didn't see Essence, but she did spot an empty table.

Skirting around people who were in line to order, her long strides carried her the short distance to the two-seater table. She arrived seconds before another woman reached it.

Cree didn't bother acknowledging her. She set her food down, placed her handbag on one of the chairs, and then planted her butt in the other. Before she could settle in, she spotted her sister entering the building.

"Hey you," Essence said as she approached, looking cute.

The short, pink plaid jacket that had the sleeves rolled up above her wrists, showed off several silver bangles. Beneath the jacket was a white tank paired with vintage jeans frayed at the ankles. Short blue pumps, which matched her jeans perfectly, covered her feet. "Hey yourself, Sexy Lady." Cree stood and hugged her sister, who was also her best friend. "You're right on time. I already have your order," she said as she reclaimed her seat. "I gotta say, Sis, I'm loving this new you."

Essence was two years older than Cree, and with them being the oldest of five, they were also the closest.

Essence grinned shyly. "Thanks. After dropping a few pounds, and then taking your advice and updating my wardrobe, I'm liking the new me too. Granted, it took me a year to listen to you, but better late than never. No more roaming around town in leggings and a T-shirt or, worse, my scrubs. Especially on my days off."

"See what happens when you listen to your little, and wiser, sister. You start looking like a sexy vixen instead of an overprotective mom of a college student."

Essence snorted and waved her off. "Yeah, yeah, whatever."

A pediatric nurse, Essence loved her job and probably put in more work hours than Cree. But lately, she'd been stepping out of her comfort zone. Though she claimed the changes had nothing to do with a man, Cree wasn't so sure, but she liked it.

As a teen mom, Essence had devoted her life to raising her son, Tray, often forgoing her own needs. It was nice seeing her doing something for herself for a change. Now that Tray had started his first year in college in Atlanta, Essence was trying to find herself and admitted it wasn't easy.

"Speaking of cute outfits, is that a new suit?" Essence asked. "You have like a trillion of them. I can never be too sure."

Cree laughed. Since she practically lived in suits, her walk-in closet was full of them in every color and style.

"Nope, I've had this one for a while, but I can't remember the last time I've worn it."

This morning she'd been going for a badass boss look and had settled on one of her favorite gray power suits. The single-button jacket had two layers of pleats that stopped just below her waist. Giving her that snatched waist look she often aimed for.

With the light-gray lace camisole beneath it, and the fitted skirt that stopped just above her knees, the outfit was sexy and sophisticated, yet professional enough for a business setting. It also showcased her best assets, her 36Ds as well as her long legs. At 5'7" she was taller than most women, and when she added her four-inch heels, she stood out in any crowd. Which had suited her well at her meetings this morning.

Small talk flowed between them as they visited, something they tried to do weekly. Essence was planning a trip to Atlanta in a few weeks for a family weekend at Clark Atlanta University where Tray attended. What didn't surprise Cree was that Jackson, Essence's best friend, was going with her. God bless that man. Cree didn't know how he maintained his staying power. He was in love with her sister, but Essence seemed clueless. Then again, maybe that had finally changed. Maybe that was why she was working on her appearance and getting out more.

"I'm thinking about moving to Atlanta," Essence announced just as Cree lifted her coffee cup.

"I guess I don't have to ask why," she said and took a careful sip of the steaming hot brew.

Cree and her siblings often accused Essence of being a helicopter parent while Tray was growing up. Granted, Cree understood her protectiveness, but Tray had turned into a responsible, independent young man. He deserved and wanted the chance to be on his own and start experiencing life without his mother hovering. At least that's what he had confided in her shortly before he left for college.

"You just don't understand," Essence said defensively while picking at her cheese Danish. "I miss him like crazy, and he hasn't even been gone two months. If I live there, at least I can see him on the weekends. And we both know I won't have a problem finding a job."

"That might be so, but what happens when he moves to a different state after he graduates? And then he moves again because of a job offer, and then another. Are you going to follow him everywhere he goes?"

"Maybe," Essence mumbled, not looking at Cree.

"What does Jackson think about it?"

Essence sighed. "He thinks, and I quote, *'Peaches, you doin' too much'*," she said, her lips twitching when she finally met Cree's eyes.

Cree laughed. "I agree, and we both know Jackson has never steered you wrong. You told me that he suggested you and him take a trip somewhere soon. Why don't you do that and stop worrying about Tray?"

"We're going on vacation in a few weeks. We're going to Atlanta."

"To see Tray," Cree countered. "That's not a vacation. Sitting on a beach, soaking up sun, and drinking cocktails with little umbrellas in them is a vacation."

Essence rolled her eyes and went back to eating. "I don't know why I tell you anything," she murmured, and Cree laughed again.

"Because I'm your bestie. Well, next to Jackson that is, but okay, I'll back off. Has Dorian been consuming all your time with her wedding plans?" Cree asked.

Their youngest sister, Dorian, had recently gotten engaged, and Essence and their mother were helping plan the New Year's Eve wedding.

"Everything is going okay, but I'm sure Dorian's going to get sick of her future mother-in-law and our mother sooner than later because..."

A scuffle at the entrance of the coffee shop caught their attention. Customers gathered around three tall individuals who were talking and laughing, and Cree groaned. She recognized all of them, but one in particular as he signed autographs.

Of all the coffee shops in the city, why'd he have to pick that one?

She had hoped when she'd seen Tristan Whitmore several

weeks ago, while she was shopping with her sister, that it would be the last time. But nope, no such luck.

"Oh boy. Don't look now, but your—"

"He's not my anything," Cree ground out. "And I think this is a good time to end our visit. I need to get going anyway. We can talk about Dorian's wedding later."

"Cree, stop. Just talk to him. It's been years, and you both deserve some closure."

"I got closure when I told him to lose my damn telephone number and to go to hell."

Cree knew she was being a jerk, but Tristan was still a sore topic with her. Seeing him again brought back too many memories, and they weren't all good.

She gathered her large bag, which doubled as a purse and laptop carrier, and then she grabbed her trash.

"I'm out of here," she said and blew her sister a kiss before walking away.

If Cree was lucky, she might be able to slip past Tristan without him seeing her. He'd been forced to retire from the NFL, the National Football League, after an injury, and she'd heard he had moved back to Chicago.

God, she hoped that wasn't true. They probably traveled in the same circles, and that would mean there was a good chance she'd run into him more than she'd prefer.

Taking advantage of the crowd that surrounded him, Cree moved around the perimeter of the space and kept her head down while making her way to the door. She had barely touched the handle before she jolted from the feel of a large hand on her hip.

She froze, but not before a zap of energy flowed through her body at his touch. She knew that touch. Hell, she'd feel that touch even if she had on three layers of clothing. Tristan had always had that effect on her.

"Cree, wait. We need to talk," he said by way of greeting. His deep baritone sent goosebumps racing over her skin. She didn't want to talk, and she sure as hell didn't want to look at him, but she had to.

When she turned to face him, anger nipped at every nerve in her body. Damn him for looking so good. He was still the finest man on the face of the planet with honey-brown skin, eyes the color of almonds with flecks of gold around his irises, and twin dimples in his cheeks.

As if knowing she was admiring his beautiful face, he amped up his smile, and she cursed under her breath.

Damn those twin dimples. The ones deep enough in his cheeks to stick her fingers in. And damn him for flashing them so freely in public knowing they were babe magnets.

"We have nothing to talk about," she spat, anger lacing the words.

"On the contrary, baby. We have a lot to discuss."

Cree turned from him and moved just beyond the threshold, but he held on to the back of her jacket while he stood in the doorway. He didn't seem to care he was blocking the entrance, keeping anyone from entering or exiting. The small crowd that had formed around him minutes ago was still there, vying for the attention of the other former NFL player whose name had slipped her mind.

As for Tristan, Cree didn't want to talk to him. That would only encourage him to keep showing up everywhere she went.

No, she needed to stay as far away from the man as possible. His presence was a hindrance to her peace of mind. It was because of him that she had trust issues, especially when it came to men. He was the reason she had taken on the motto— don't let anyone get too close because in the end they'll only betray you.

"The old Cree didn't run from anything," he said, his voice lowered. "Yet, you've run from me twice in a matter of weeks."

Her jaw clenched and unclenched. "The old Cree would've already kneed you in the balls to make you release my jacket. Either let me go or..."

Tristan flinched, then quickly released her jacket and chuckled. "I see you're still mean as hell." The words weren't spoken in a negative way. There was humor in his tone and in his eyes. "Please," he said, all humor wiped from his face. "I really do need to talk to you."

Cree searched his eyes and saw the sincerity in them. She almost gave in to his request until she remembered—she hated him.

"There's nothing for us to discuss. As a matter of fact, forget you ever saw me, and if you see me out and about, don't even look at me.

"And on that note, goodbye, Tristan."

Now all she had to do was forget she'd ever seen him. Which might be easier said than done.

Chapter Two

Tristan pounded his hand on the metal doorframe as he watched Cree sachet away.

Dammit. The woman was still as mean as a rattlesnake.

At least this time he wasn't literally running down the street to catch her. Doing that once a few weeks ago had been enough. Not only had he run after her, but he had caught her just in time before she pulled away in her car. Surprisingly, the passenger door had been unlocked, and he had hopped right into the front seat of her SUV.

Tristan still couldn't believe he'd done that, but he was determined to talk to her after not having seen her in years. However, Cree, being Cree, hadn't seemed phased. She'd kept driving, giving him the silent treatment in the process.

Most people would've pulled over and told him to get out. Not her. Instead, she drove to her office. Once there, she pulled into a parking spot and *then* told him to get the hell out. Not only that, but she'd also told him that if he came near her again, she'd file a restraining order against him.

"Excuse me," a man, who was standing outside the coffee shop, said and jarred Tristan out of his thoughts. The guy frowned and pointed at him. "Aren't you Tristan Whitmore?"

Suddenly not in the mood for fans, autographs, or anything else for that matter, Tristan stepped back into the building and turned abruptly. Unfortunately, when he did, he slammed into a woman, and her iced coffee landed on his chest and dripped down the front of his body.

He leaped back. "Oh, shit." The coldness from the ice sent a violent shiver through his body, and he sucked in a breath. Her cup had landed on the floor while the front of his clothes was completely covered with her iced coffee.

"Oh, no!" the woman cried. "I'm so sorry."

She used the napkins in her hands and feverishly wiped at the wet spots on his shirt, but when her hand absently went lower, he jerked away while gently grabbing her wrist.

"I got it," he ground out and watched as her face turned beet red. He felt like a jerk and took some of the bite out of his tone when he added, "Thanks anyway."

She covered her face with her hands. "God, I'm so embarrassed," she said, then lowered her hands. "I feel awful, but I couldn't get out of the way because you turned too quickly. I'll take care of your dry cleaning if you want. I'm really sorry."

"No, this is all on me," Tristan said. "Literally," he added and chuckled. "Let me replace your drink for you."

"Thank you, but instead of the drink, can I have your autograph for my boyfriend? He's a huge fan, and then you and I can call it even."

"That works too," Tristan said as the woman pulled a notepad and pen from her purse and handed it to him.

She flashed a grateful smile. "My boyfriend's name is Stanley."

Tristan hurried to scribble a quick message and signed his name. He handed back the notebook.

"Sorry about your coffee," he said, trying to act cool despite his beige dress shirt having a big wet spot on it and his brown pants sticking to him.

"It's okay. I've been trying to cut back on caffeine anyway. I just hate that your clothes are ruined," she said, and again, he assured her that it was okay.

Once she left, and one of the servers started cleaning up the mess on the floor, Tristan was stopped by another woman.

"Essence, it's been too long," he said and gave her a side hug while she kissed his cheek.

She smiled at him and said, "It's always good seeing you, Tristan, and I'm glad you're up and moving around. As for Cree," she nodded her head toward the door that Cree had left through, "don't give up on her. You know how stubborn she is, but I think you two should talk."

She backed toward the door as he nodded.

"I agree, and we will."

"Great and good luck," she tossed over her shoulder before leaving the building.

When he turned around, his brother, Quincy, was there.

"Are you done messing around?" Quincy asked with a wicked grin on his face.

Tristan was three years younger, but anyone could tell they were related despite their physical differences. Both had the same skin tone with a similar eye color and stood at 6'3 with broad shoulders, but that's where their similarities stopped. Tristan was more muscular thanks to his rigorous workouts while playing football. He also was clean-shaven and dressed more casually, while Quincy had a full beard and could almost always be found wearing a suit.

"You haven't been here five minutes, yet you've managed to

ruin the day of two women," his brother cracked. "Cree looked as if she could murder you, and that other woman has to go without her afternoon coffee. What do you have to say for yourself?"

"Man, shut up," Tristan grumbled.

Laughing, Quincy held up a container that held two drinks, and in the other hand was a paper bag. "I ordered for you, and Jamal saved us a table. Are you staying or going home? You look like a wet dog."

Tristan ignored his brother's taunt. Yes, he looked a mess, but he didn't have time to run home and then come back. Since he'd been the one to ask to meet up, it would be rude to bail on them.

"Nah, I'll hang out," he said.

Once he went home and changed, he planned to pay Cree a visit at work. She couldn't get rid of him that easily. They were going to talk, and they were going to talk today. He wasn't taking *no* for an answer no matter how much she threatened him.

Tristan unbuttoned his shirt, glad he had a T-shirt beneath it. Granted, the T-shirt was wet, but it was darker in color and didn't look as bad.

As he followed Quincy to the dining area, a couple of people stopped him for an autograph. He had to admit these days that the requests were a nice boost to his ego. Months ago, he had learned the injury he had sustained during a football game shortly before Christmas was career-ending. He'd been devastated. Playing in the NFL had been a dream come true, and he thought when he retired, it would be by choice. Instead, he'd been forced to retire because despite his incredible recovery, he was no longer able to play at the same professional level.

"Man, you sure know how to make an entrance," his best friend, Jamal, said when they joined him at the table.

"I guess some things never change," Quincy added. "Even as a kid, Tristan wanted to be the center of attention. I thought for sure when he moved back here from Philly that he'd be leaving his fans behind. Apparently not. Chicago still loves him even though he abandoned them to go and play for another team."

It was true. Tristan had only played for Chicago during his first season in the NFL, but then Philly made him an offer he couldn't refuse. For years, he lived his dream, even though it hadn't been for the home team. He had hoped to one day play for Chicago again, but Philly had been good to him.

Now that he was no longer in the league, and had moved back to Chicago, he hadn't known what type of reception he'd receive. But if he was honest, there was only one person whose opinion he cared about right now, and she wanted nothing to do with him.

As they talked and drank their coffees, Tristan couldn't help but think about his interaction with Cree. It had been years since they'd had their disagreement, and clearly, she wasn't over it. How the hell was he going to make things right with her if she wouldn't even give him the time of day?

"I didn't know Cree could get any more beautiful," Jamal said. "I almost didn't recognize her, and that sexy ass haircut only enhances her beauty."

"Yeah, that was the only difference because that slamming body of hers was still as—"

"I suggest you shut up now if you want to keep your teeth," Tristan growled.

Quincy chuckled. "Touchy, touchy."

Tristan knew his brother was trying to get a rise out of him, but still, he didn't like men noticing Cree's body. Especially since her sexy hourglass figure could be distracting enough to make a man walk into oncoming traffic without realizing it.

That definitely hadn't changed. Add her sassy haircut, gorgeous face, and self-confidence that made people take notice, and you had the most alluring woman who ever existed.

Having played professional football for so many years, he'd had access to his share of women. Yet, they were no comparison to Cree Priestly. She was the complete package of brains and beauty with just the right amount of sass. The guys were right. She'd only gotten more gorgeous over the years.

"So, I guess Cree still wants nothing to do with you, huh?" Quincy said between bites of his ham and cheese sandwich. "You can't much blame her, though. What you did was underhanded and downright inconsiderate."

"*Dude*, it wasn't underhanded at all," Jamal defended. "Yes, our boy could've handled the situation differently, but he had to do what he had to do. And you of all people should be happy he did. Otherwise, you might not have that cushy CEO position at his nonprofit."

As the two argued back and forth, Tristan sipped his black coffee while remembering his time with Cree. He'd been twenty-one, she'd been twenty-four, and being with an older woman had been a fantasy come true. Even back then, she hadn't been easy to get along with, but he knew meeting her had been fate. Especially when he'd learned she was a sports agent. She ended up being his agent... as well as his lover.

Tristan pinched the bridge of his nose as the memories flooded his mind all at once. They'd both been so young, thrown into a world with grown folks, but Cree could handle herself. She'd been a badass even back then, and he knew she'd only gotten more incredible over the years. She had always carried herself as a boss-lady, even when he unintentionally pulled the rug from under her.

Quincy was right. Tristan had done her wrong, but it had been for a good reason. Still, he messed up. If he could go back in time and make different choices, he would. He didn't realize what he had until she was gone. Now, he wanted her back in every way possible.

Tristan jerked when he was hit in the face with a wadded-up napkin.

"Are you listening to anything we're saying?" his brother asked, frowning.

"No, I wasn't listening because I'm sure you two aren't talking about shit."

"Actually, I was saying Jamal's uncle is selling one of his commercial properties located near downtown," Quincy said. "We need more office space for the nonprofit, and I think his building could work. Not only is it a good size, but it's also large enough to rent out part of it."

The Whitmore Foundation held a special spot in Tristan's heart. He and Quincy had started the nonprofit years after Tristan had joined the NFL. Growing up, their parents had struggled financially to keep them in various sports, and he had vowed that, once he had money, he'd give back to his community.

There were some talented kids out there who often didn't get a chance to compete because of a lack of funds. From registration fees to being able to buy uniforms, there was an expense for families. Which was why he'd come up with the idea for their Foundation to provide financial assistance to underserved youth who play sports.

Quincy was doing a great job running the organization, and their younger sister oversaw fundraising efforts. Thanks to them, the nonprofit was thriving. So if Quincy, who was tight with the budget, felt they needed more space, Tristan would support his request. Although purchasing a property wouldn't be his first choice, he trusted his brother's judgment.

Tristan listened as they told him about the three-story brick building and surrounding small businesses. That included a spa on one side and a real estate office on the other. As for size, it sounded perfect for their needs. All he needed to do was make time to go and see it.

Suddenly hungry, he dug through the paper bag. Instead of grabbing the sandwich, he pulled out the blueberry muffin.

Eating the sweet treat reminded him that he no longer had to stick to a strict eating plan. Had it not been for his injury last season, he'd be at practice right now, getting ready for the Philly's season opener. There were days Tristan still struggled with the fact that he couldn't play football anymore. He'd never get to hear the roar of the fans in the stands while he charged past some of the biggest, baddest defensive linemen in the game.

God, he already missed the life he'd once had. All of it, even the days where every part of his body hurt from all the tackles he endured.

"Your life isn't over just because you're not on the football field," his best friend said as if reading his mind. "You'll always be one of the world's greatest running backs to play the game. Not as good as me, of course." He laughed, and Tristan shook his head and snorted.

He and Jamal had grown up together and had even played peewee football together. Though they attended different colleges, and their paths to the NFL had been slightly different, they made it. They had both achieved their lifelong dream, but while Tristan was in the league for almost thirteen years, Jamal had only lasted six.

"The league loves you, man. I'm sure there's a team out there that wants you in their camp in one capacity or another."

Tristan nodded. He was at a crossroads in his life, constantly thinking about his future and trying to decide which direction to take. The guys didn't know it yet, but he had already heard from two NFL teams. They wanted him to consider being their running back coach.

So far, it was being kept quiet that those teams were looking at him as part of their coaching search. However, it was only a matter of time before the news would hit the media. Assuming they didn't already know about that, as well as a few other opportunities.

Tristan wasn't looking forward to tomorrow or the next day because that's when it would be announced he had fired his agent. A sought-after agent who never got fired and was usually the first to cut ties from clients.

All the more reason why Tristan needed to talk to Cree as soon as possible. He needed her help, and he already knew it wasn't going to be easy to get it.

Chapter Three

Cree thought the ten-minute walk back to the office would be all she needed to calm down. It wasn't. No, she would need hours or maybe even days to get over her encounter with Tristan. The man still had the ability to throw her off-balance, and knowing that drove her nuts.

Seeing him again sparked too many emotions—surprise, anger, and even lust. The last one bugged her the most because she'd only been in his presence for five minutes. Five frickin' minutes! Yet, that was all it took for her body to respond to him, to crave him, and to recall all they once shared.

Tristan was even more gorgeous than she remembered. The sight of those soulful eyes, as well as those tempting, masterful lips that had brought her immense pleasure back in the day, haunted her even now.

She almost groaned. Why'd he have to be finer than he'd been years ago? Why couldn't he be sporting bloodshot eyes, missing all his front teeth, and have a beer belly that hung to his knees? Instead, he was every woman's fantasy. Tall, dark, and downright gorgeous with a body designed for pleasing a woman.

Cree hadn't missed the attention he had garnered from those in the coffee shop. Tristan might've worn a helmet on the football field, but between television commercials, magazine covers, and a few cameos in movies, he had gained notoriety with both sexes. Not only was he handsome, but he was also charming.

She was curious to see what he'd end up doing now that he'd been forced to retire from the game he loved. No doubt he'd be in hot demand since he had so much going for him— looks, a positive personality, and he was endearing, giving him all he needed to influence the hardest of hearts.

Yeah, he was marketable, and he'd be flooded with opportunities. Cree wondered if he would...

Dammit!

Who cared what he did? Not her! As far as she was concerned, Tristan could fall off the face of the earth, and she wouldn't go looking for him.

Okay, maybe that was too extreme. She didn't wish him harm. She just didn't want anything to do with him. He had hurt her too much. Betrayed her when she was vulnerable, and he probably had no clue as to just how much he had crushed her spirit.

Everyone always thought she was the strong one. The one who was unshakable, and for the most part, she was. Yet there had been a time in her life when she had counted on Tristan. She'd needed him in more ways than one, and he'd let her down.

But that was the past, and the mistakes she'd made with him would never be repeated.

At least that's what she kept telling herself as she stomped down the street. She was no longer the young and naive twenty-four-year-old who thought she knew everything about everything.

Nope. Now she was a grown-ass woman who knew better than to go against her gut feelings. She also knew better than to open her heart and trust a man the way she had trusted Tristan. The asshole had gotten past her defenses, but she wouldn't let that happen again.

"Never again," she mumbled as she followed a few people into her office building. She couldn't let thoughts of Tristan consume her. She had moved on, and there was no way she would allow him back into her life in any capacity.

She marched across the shiny travertine floors and headed to the bank of elevators. There were numerous businesses that operated out of the building, and the lobby was bustling with people coming and going. However, she kept her attention straight ahead. She needed to get up to her office so she could decompress before her next meeting.

A few minutes later, Cree exited the elevator on the twenty-first floor, where their law office was located. She strolled past a large, plush waiting room, several cubicles, and a couple of conference rooms until she entered the partners' office area. The suite of offices was set in back, away from the small waiting area she was currently standing in.

As she approached the long counter, Shantel, their executive assistant, who was on the telephone, lifted her finger, silently asking Cree to wait.

"Yes, sir. I'll make sure Mr. Ellis gets the message. Have a good day.

"Sorry about that, Cree," Shantel said after ending the call. "You just missed a call from Mr. Charleston. He had to cancel his three o'clock meeting with you."

Now that was the best news she'd heard all day. She wasn't

in the mood to meet with a potential new client. "Did he reschedule?"

"Yes," Shantel said slowly as she glanced down at her calendar. "He rescheduled for next Thursday and apologized for the short notice. He has to fly to New York—family emergency."

Cree nodded. "Okay. That gives me the afternoon to catch up on some work."

Before walking away, she told Shantel that she was not to be disturbed unless it was an emergency. She had a dinner meeting later. Until then, she'd see how much work she could get through.

Two hours later, Cree dropped back against her leather desk chair and released a long sigh. It had been days since she'd been able to get through any amount of work without being interrupted.

"This is good," she murmured into the quietness of the space.

Her large corner office was one of her favorite places to spend time, even if it was for working. It was functional, while also being relaxing with very light blue, almost white, walls and oak hardwood floors. Behind her desk were floor-to-ceiling bookshelves that not only held law books, but numerous awards and keepsakes. To her left was a wall of windows with a view of equally tall buildings, and across from her desk was a sitting area. It held a comfortable sofa with end tables and a straight-backed upholstered chair. She also had her own bathroom. Though small, it offered a convenience she appreciated.

Feeling at peace, Cree laid her head back against the chair and rested her eyes. She had almost dozed off when her desk phone beeped.

Yawning, she sat forward and picked up the receiver. "Yes, Shantel."

"Sorry to bother you, but you have a visitor—Tristan Whitmore."

Cree's breath caught as shock charged through her, and then she pounded her hand on the desk.

Damn him. What part of *stay away* from her had he not understood?

Then again, who was she kidding? Saying no to Tristan or telling him not to do something was like daring him to do it. A lot of his success had to do with the fact that he didn't take no for an answer, and Cree telling him to stay away was like holding out a red flag in a bullfight. He'd charge forward just to provoke her.

Clearly, he'd forgotten who he was dealing with. He couldn't just snap his fingers and expect her to fall at his feet. And if he thought that's what she'd do, he had another thing coming.

"Tell Mr. Whitmore I'm busy, and if he wants to meet with me, then make an appointment. And when he tries to make an appointment, make sure he understands I'm busy for the next twenty years."

Silence greeted her on the other end of the phone line before Shantel burst out laughing. "Yes, ma'am," she said and then disconnected the call.

That ought to get rid of him.

Cree went back to work. After another hour, she slipped her feet back into her high heels that were under the desk and stood. She'd gotten stiff from all the sitting, but in turn, she was able to clear out her inbox. Now she needed to move her body some and maybe even get out of the office a minute.

Twisting back and forth at the waist, she stretched her back, then reached up high for another stretch. After breathing in and out a few times, she let her arms drop down to her sides.

With her muscles feeling loose, she grabbed the two padded envelopes that needed mailing and headed out of her office.

She strolled down the short hallway, and as she entered the waiting area, Cree spotted two men sitting on opposite sides of the space. However, there was only one who met and held her gaze, and Cree pulled up short.

Tristan. The last person she expected to see. Had he really been here for the past hour?

He stood to his imposing height, and her breath stalled in her throat as he buttoned his suit jacket. At well over six feet tall, the man was dressed to impress and looking as if he came to play hardball. Gone were the dress shirt and pants from earlier. In its place was a navy-blue suit that screamed wealth, and no doubt had been tailored specifically for his drool-worthy body.

The man looked larger than life standing there, and it was taking every bit of strength Cree had not to walk up to him and kiss him senseless.

Yeah, that wouldn't be smart at all. Still, she was tempted.

She swallowed hard as she struggled to keep her gaze from traveling over his impressive physique. Impossible. There was no woman alive who could see this man and not do a double take. Hell, they probably wouldn't be able to take their eyes off him period.

Yeah, he was that fine, and the suit only added to his imposing masculinity.

Her gaze did a slow glide over his extra broad shoulders that looked strong enough to hold up a twenty-story building. Then there were his ridiculously wide chest and biceps almost as big as her thighs.

But in this suit, every part of him seemed magnified. Except his waist. His shoulders tapered down to a narrow waist. She didn't have to look beneath the clothes to know he still had eight-pack abs.

And those thighs? Lord have mercy. It was no wonder he was one of the best running backs to play the game. His pants highlighted his powerful thighs and long, super long legs.

Immediately, memories of him holding her up against the wall as if she weighed nothing, while thrusting in and out of her, flooded her mind. Sex with him had always been intense, hot, and beyond satisfying as he brought her to one orgasm after another.

Cree shook the memory free and realized Tristan's confident steps were bringing him closer.

"Hello, Cree," he said when he stood in front of her, and the sound of his voice was deep and as sexy as the rest of him.

Cree heard Shantel whimper, and she couldn't much blame her. This was all part of the power that Tristan willed over unsuspecting women.

His gaze swept the length of Cree's body before returning to her eyes. Then he held up a thick manila envelope in his right hand, which was when she noted the bling on one of his fingers and more around his wrist.

His wealth was showing on every part of his body, and it all looked good on him.

Tristan moved even closer and lowered his voice. "We can either talk now, or we can have this conversation over dinner tonight. Your choice."

Chapter Four

Tristan had known it wouldn't be easy to get some alone time with Cree, and he'd been right. The way she was glowering at him told him all he needed to know. She was pissed, and he should be very afraid.

So when she huffed out an exasperated breath, handed the receptionist some envelopes, and suddenly turned on her sky-high heels, he just stood there. Should he follow her and risk her wrath? Or should he leave and rethink his *Win-Cree-Back* campaign?

"Go!" the lady at the desk, Shantel, whisper-shouted and shooed him with her hands to follow Cree.

"Right. On it," he said and gave her a head nod before rushing after Cree who seemed to be speed-walking.

His gaze immediately followed the rhythmic motion of her gorgeous ass in that tight skirt. And those long, shapely legs? One of her greatest assets that he had missed. Yes, he wanted her back in his life in every way that she'd been years ago, and he especially wanted to get reacquainted with her luscious curves. The woman had the body of a goddess, and...

No. Stop.

He had to stay focused. Before he moved on to phase two of *Win-Cree-Back*, he needed to get her in his corner again. He needed her to represent him with the numerous offers that had come his way.

Cree slowed near the last door on the right before entering the office, and Tristan half expected her to slam the door in his face. She didn't. Instead, she waited until he crossed the threshold before she slammed the door and whirled on him.

"What part of *leave me the hell alone* don't you understand?" she growled. Like for real growled as anger seeped from her pores, and Tristan was fairly sure that was smoke coming from her ears.

And damn if she wasn't turning him on in every way possible. If that made him a jerk, oh well. Her take-no-bullshit was one of the first things that had attracted him to her in the first place. That and her long shapely legs that made him weak in the knees whenever he saw them, like today.

But right now, it was her attitude and her fragrance pulling him in. It was as if the madder she got, the more pronounced her lavender and vanilla scent intensified. If he didn't think she'd knock him the hell out, he'd bury his nose into the crook of her neck for a better whiff.

"We need to talk," Tristan finally said, meeting her dark gaze as he reminded himself of why he was there.

As he stared into her gorgeous eyes, something familiar stirred inside of him. Excitement. Connection. Desire. He wanted more than anything to pick up where they'd left off before their relationship exploded into a trillion little pieces.

Though it might be impossible, he was determined to rekindle their relationship. He wanted to prove she could trust and depend on him again. Unfortunately, Cree wasn't the forgiving type. Still, he was going to give it a shot and achieve the first part of his plan. After that, even if it took the rest of his life, he was going to win her heart again.

He had to. He had never loved another woman the way he loved Cree. What he once felt for her was like nothing he had ever experienced, and that was still the case. Besides being with her, he'd only had one long-term relationship. A relationship that had lasted a year but had never been as fulfilling as his and Cree's. In the end, that woman dumped him because she accused him of being emotionally unavailable. Telling him that he needed to go back to the woman who clearly held his heart because it wasn't her.

Tristan hadn't been able to argue with her. Cree had his heart, still, and didn't even know it.

"We have nothing to talk about," Cree ground out and put space between them. "Tristan, I want nothing to do with you. Why can't you get that through your thick head? Whatever game you're playing, I want nothing to do with it."

"I stopped playing games the day I took a direct hit to my knee in one of the most important games of my life," he said through gritted teeth as frustration stirred within him at the memory and the mental and physical pain he had endured. He'd already had knee issues, but in that game, he had suffered a major tear of his ACL and a mild tear of his MCL. And just like that, his career had been over.

"So yeah, my game playing days are over. I'm here on business. I want you to represent me," he said, getting right to the point of his visit.

He watched a slew of emotions flit across her face as her gaze went from his eyes to his injured knee and back to his eyes. She knew. She knew what he'd been through during the last nine months of recovering. Which had prompted her to not only send him his favorite dessert—Chicago style Garrett Popcorn—but she had included a card. *Hurry and get well*, it had said. Out of all the well-wishes he had received during that time, hers was the one that meant the most.

Cree wasn't known for being empathetic or sympathetic for that matter, but for her to send a handwritten note was huge. It told him that she still cared, though she'd never admit it.

"Cree, I no longer have an agent, and I need someone to read through a few offers I've received recently."

Time stood still as she stared at him as if he had lost his mind. He was mentally ready for whatever she threw his way. He had no intention of backing off, and he was prepared to fight dirty if necessary.

He needed her, and he wanted them to be back in each other's life again.

"I'm not a sports agent, Tristan, but you know that. And even if I was, I wouldn't represent you, but I'm sure you know that too. Hell, I'd change careers before I ever took you on as a client again. So, if that's what you came here for, our conversation is done. Get out," she spat and opened her office door.

Tristan sighed loudly and set the huge manila envelope on her tidy desk. He had received a couple of staffing offers from different teams, as well as endorsement deals from companies over the past few days.

He had no idea which he'd agree to if any. Now that he was back in Chicago, that's where he wanted to stay. So whatever deals he took had to fit into the new life he wanted to build for himself.

He folded his arms across his chest and leveled Cree with an unwavering stare. "I'm not leaving until you say yes."

There was another growl from her, and she balled one of her fists.

"Tristan, you are working my last nerve," she bit out quietly. "I told you we have nothing to discuss, and I mean it. My answer is no to anything you want from me."

"Sorry to interrupt," a male's voice sounded before the man appeared in the doorway.

Tristan smiled inside when he recognized one of the partners at the firm. He had done his research before coming and remembered the guy from his photo on their website.

The guy strolled into the office with a huge smile on his face and his hand outstretched.

"Mr. Whitmore, I'm Warren Ellis, one of the partners here. I'm a huge fan, and it's a pleasure to meet you."

Tristan shook his hand. "The pleasure is mine, Attorney Ellis."

"Please, call me Warren."

Tristan nodded. "And please call me Tristan. Mr. Whitmore is my father," he said on a chuckle as he did a quick glance at Cree.

He had to bite down on his lower lip to keep from smiling. The daggers she was shooting at him with her eyes was almost comical, but laughing would only make things worse between them.

Yeah, he was an asshole because he was enjoying this too much. He couldn't have planned this moment better if he'd tried. Now that one of the partners had seen him, it would be harder for her not to take him on as a client.

"Again, I'm sorry to interrupt," Warren said, his gray-eyed gaze bouncing from Tristan to Cree and back again. "But I heard you were in the building and had to stop by to introduce myself." Warren lingered and talked football for a few minutes longer before backing out the door that Cree was still holding on to. "I hope to see you around," Warren said before side-eyeing Cree on his way out.

What the hell was that all about?

A wave of protectiveness gripped Tristan, and he struggled

to keep his mouth shut. Something was up between those two, and whatever it was it wasn't good.

When Warren left, Cree's shoulders sagged, and she closed the door. Leaning against it, she released a loud breath.

"Why did he look at you like that?" Tristan asked quietly, keeping his attention on Cree's face. He didn't miss the vulnerability in her eyes, but just as quickly as it appeared, it disappeared.

She folded her arms across her chest, and the move brought attention to the swell of her full breasts peeking from above her camisole.

Tristan swallowed hard as memories of her glorious, naked breasts filled his mind. The woman had a nice rack that went great with the rest of her perfect body. A body that he was once very familiar with.

But he needed to stop thinking about her body and focus on her and why he was there.

"I hate you so much right now," she said, her voice low.

She didn't answer his question, but Tristan planned to bring it back around at some point. If not today, then another day. If she was having trouble with this guy, he wanted to know. Especially if it was something he could help with.

The fight might've gone out of her tone, but the disgust radiating in her eyes matched her words.

His arrogant ass refused to believe she hated him. Yes, she was clearly still mad at how things went down between them years ago, but he didn't think she hated him. If she was anyone else, even if she was mad, she'd sign him on as a client and then just charge him an arm and a leg to represent him.

But considering her reaction to him weeks ago and then again today, Tristan couldn't help wondering if there was something else keeping her from forgiving him. Thirteen years was a long time to hold a grudge for firing her as his agent.

He pushed away from the desk and approached her. He needed her to see the sincerity in his eyes. "Cree, I am sorry about how things went down between us. I have said it over and over again. I hated the way I handled the situation back then. I was young and dumb, but please know my decision was business. It wasn't personal. *Never* personal."

He almost added that he was still in love with her and would never intentionally do anything to hurt her, but he kept that admission to himself.

She closed her eyes as she rubbed the back of her neck. There'd been a time when he would've reached out and worked the kinks out of her neck. Too bad he had lost those privileges. He loved having his hands on every part of her.

When she reopened her eyes, he said, "I know I'm the last person you want to see, let alone represent, but I need a lawyer to look over those offers." He pointed to her desk.

She didn't look at the envelope. Instead, she stared at him with an unreadable expression on her pretty face. His gaze devoured her flawless bronze skin, doe-shaped eyes, short-bridge nose, and full, kissable lips. She might be angry, and even frustrated with him, but she was still the most beautiful woman in the world to him.

"I can't represent you, Tristan. Apparently, you have forgotten how you fired me the last time. Without notice I might add. You didn't give a damn that you were my main client. All that mattered to you was whether you had a new agent who promised you the world. Then you kicked me and my agency to the curb like I meant *nothing*!" she snarled as she pointed at herself, her finger jabbing into her chest as her words got louder. "Like I hadn't been the first person to take a chance on you... a nobody."

She moved away from the door and started pacing her office, clearly trying to regain her composure. Tristan kept quiet. She had every right to be pissed at him. Though things didn't happen quite the way she was recalling, the fact was—he had signed with a different agent.

He'd been twenty-one, almost twenty-two, and he'd had an opportunity to sign with the most sought-after agent in the world. No matter how he tried to explain the importance of that to her, Cree refused to listen. She had taken it personal instead of seeing it as a business transaction.

While that had been the case for her, he'd seen the move as a win for not just him but for them. Especially since she was a part of him—the woman he had planned to spend the rest of his life with.

But what she was failing to take into consideration right now was that they weren't kids anymore. He wasn't at the beginning of his career trying to make a name for himself while also wanting to provide financially for his family. No. He was wealthy enough to live comfortably for the rest of his life without accepting any of the offers on the table.

What she also didn't understand was that he wanted her to represent him going forward because he owed her. She was right. She had taken a chance on him all those years ago, and he never forgot that.

Cree pulled him out of his thoughts when she stopped a couple of feet from him. "My answer is no, but I'd be happy to connect you with one of the other partners here."

Tristan had expected her to say no and a few other things, but he wasn't taking no for an answer.

He stepped forward and slid his arm around her waist, bringing her flush against his body. Desire spiraled through him, but he pushed it down for now.

"That's not going to work for me," he finally said, his voice gruffer than intended.

Surprisingly, Cree didn't push him away even though their

faces were inches apart. It was taking all his self-control not to lower his head and kiss her tempting, red lips. He couldn't. There was too much at stake to ruin it with temporary pleasure. Instead, he was keeping his eyes on the big prize—her. Having *all* of her again.

"Cree, it's either you or nobody."

Chapter Five

Cree swallowed hard as she glanced into the intense dark eyes of the man she once loved.

Tristan's nearness was wreaking havoc on her nerves. His familiar scent, his hands on her body, combined with the way her heart rate spiked, made it clear he was still a temptation impossible to ignore.

If either of them moved even an inch, their lips would be touching, and if that happened, there'd be no going back. There was no way she could kiss him and not want more. It had always been like that. He'd been her one and only addiction in life. One that had been almost impossible to break.

From the day they'd met outside of a popular club in Chicago, she'd found Tristan irresistible. She'd always been drawn to him. Their chemistry inside and out of the bedroom was stronger than anything she had ever experienced. Like some type of impenetrable gravitational pull that drew them together with such force.

God help her because she was feeling it now. She wanted to kiss him more than she wanted her next breath. Just a taste.

"I mean it, Cree. I don't want anyone but you," Tristan said, and the double-meaning wasn't lost on her.

And just like that, she felt as if she was being doused with a big bucket of ice water.

She took a giant step back, forcing Tristan's arm to drop from around her waist.

What the heck? Why'd she let him touch her and breathe the same air as her?

Suddenly she wanted to strangle this infuriating man. He was lucky it wouldn't be professional for her to wrap her hands around his thick neck and squeeze. But the last thing she needed was to have the media showing up, claiming she killed the future Hall of Famer.

"You are in no position to make demands," she snapped and gave him a wide berth as she moved to her desk and dropped down into her chair.

There was no way in hell she'd represent him. The nerve of him to think she could just forgive and forget.

"The only reason you're in my office is because I didn't want to make a scene in the waiting area. In here, though? I have no problem telling you to go straight to hell. I don't want you as a client. I don't even want you breathing the same air as me. As a matter of fact, in case I haven't made myself clear, I. Don't. Want. You. Anywhere. Near. Me."

Tristan sat in one of the chairs in front of her desk and looked as unbothered as usual with her mini rant. Which was another reason why she couldn't stand him. He was the only person she'd ever met who didn't buckle under her tirades. Or in this case, her rejection. Instead, he was always tolerant, as if she was a brat, and he was patiently waiting for her to stop with the theatrics. He'd said as much on more than one occasion.

"I'm serious, Tristan," Cree said with less venom in her tone. "I want nothing to do with you."

Then she thought about Warren. No doubt the guy was curious about Tristan's reason for being there, and he probably could feel the tension between them. Even Tristan had noticed the look Warren had given her on his way out the door. A look that said, *Don't mess this up. We want his business.*

Yet, Cree had to take care of herself because Tristan was a detriment to her peace of mind... and her heart.

"What happened to your super fly agent who you left me for?" she asked.

Tristan sat back in the chair and stretched out his legs, and Cree didn't miss the way he winced. Was he still having knee problems?

She would never forget that infamous Sunday when she'd been watching his football game, saw him crash hard to the ground, and not get up. Her heart had stopped in that instance, and she prayed he'd get up.

But when the television cameras zoomed in on him, lying in agony in the end zone, Cree knew it was bad. Excruciating pain marred his handsome face, and it was as if she could feel his agony. That had been one of few times when she wanted to rush to his side and make sure he was all right.

It was then she realized he still meant something to her. That he was still...

Cree shook the rest of that thought out of her head just as Tristan said, "I fired him."

"Why?" Cree could be mad all she wanted, but she couldn't stop the curiosity flowing through her.

Why now? Why would he fire the most sought-after agent after all these years?

She'd known Tristan had moved back to Chicago, but why was he seeking new representation when he'd had the best? Yes, she could admit Ralph Dawson had been, and still was, one of the best agents in the business, and everyone knew it.

Even she was in awe of some of the sizable, history-making contracts Ralph had negotiated. Most clients wouldn't dream of cutting ties with the man.

"There are thousands of agents and entertainment lawyers," Cree continued. "Again... Why me? Is it because you haven't tortured me enough? Oh, I know, you want to hire me, and then when a better agent or entertainment lawyer comes along, you want to dump me again."

"Cree, baby, you know it wasn't like that, and I want you because you're perfect for me," Tristan said, his unwavering gaze dared her to contradict him.

Cree huffed out a breath and ignored the last part of his statement. Yeah, she understood why he cut her loose years ago for a more experienced agent. She also understood it was business. The problem was how he'd done it. She found out he had signed with Ralph by watching Sports Center one night.

To say she'd been shocked was an understatement. At first, she thought the announcer had gotten the details wrong because there was no way Tristan would get another agent without first informing her.

That night, when she confronted him, he admitted to it. Admitted Ralph had been pursuing him for weeks before Tristan met with him. Supposedly he hadn't known how to tell her that he had signed with the guy.

An apology had barely been out of his mouth before Cree swung at him. He dodged her punch, but that didn't stop her from shooting a wine glass at him. Thankfully, his reflexes had been on point because he had ducked just in time.

No one had ever betrayed her like that, and she'd felt like a fool for not seeing it coming. She immediately shut down her emotions. She hadn't wanted to hear anything Tristan had to say. Especially when he professed his love for her while her small sports agency was on the verge of crumbling. She might've had other clients, but Tristan was her highest earning one, and he knew that. She'd needed him to help her business stay afloat, at least until she added more athletes to her client roster.

It hadn't helped matters that Cree had been young and full of herself. Her ego had taken a huge hit and so had her bottom line. She'd had so much going on in her life that the timing couldn't have been worse.

"Cree, at least look at the offers and see what's at stake." Tristan nodded at the manila envelope that he had set on her desk. "I'm sure you'll agree adding me to your client list will not only be beneficial to you, but also to this firm. I'd imagine reeling in another client, who can bring in *millions* to the organization, would be worth considering. Besides, I've never known you to turn down a major opportunity."

She narrowed her eyes at him. He knew her too well. Her partnership at the firm was solid, but that didn't mean she'd ever stop bringing in more clients. Which in turn meant more revenue and profit for the agency.

With that thought, and the fact Warren had seen Tristan in her office, she needed to at least consider Tristan's request.

Cree pulled the documents from the envelope and silently skimmed the papers. Quickly taking in the terms, deliverables, and compensation before doing the same with the next two.

Damn this man. If she signed him, the endorsement offers alone would bring in over ten million in revenue to the agency. Which would be great toward their bottom line. He'd also be the only NFL, or former NFL, player signed with them at this time.

Of course, she'd known he was big time now, but this? He wasn't even playing football anymore, yet the money these organizations were willing to pay him was impressive.

"Take a look at the last two offers," he said, and she shuffled the papers around until she reached what she was looking for.

Cree skimmed both, struggling not to react to the minimal terms and clauses that were definitely in Tristan's favor. And the dollar amounts? Unbelievable.

"So, you think you're the shit now that all these organizations are throwing money at you, huh?" Cree said, struggling to hide a smile.

She could be mad at him while also being proud and impressed with what he had accomplished over the years. He'd been one of the best running backs in the league, and these offers reflected that and more.

Tristan grinned and then chuckled. "What can I say? I'm just good like that."

They both laughed, and Cree shook her head before sobering.

"Congratulations, Tristan. I mean that. You worked hard to get to where you are today, and you deserve all the love coming your way."

He nodded. "Thanks, baby. That means a lot coming from you."

Him calling her *baby* was like hearing fingernails scrape across a chalkboard. When he betrayed her, he lost the right to refer to her by a pet name.

"With that said, I can't represent you, Tristan. We have history, and things I allowed to happen back then can never happen now. I'm at a different place in my life professionally and personally. Besides, I'll never forget how you treated me."

He huffed out a long breath and unfolded his tall frame from the upholstered chair. Then he walked around the desk and perched on the edge of it before looking at her.

"What's it going to take for you to forgive me?" he asked, watching her intently with those alluring eyes.

"If you stay away from me, I'll forgive you," she said with a straight face.

Tristan chuckled, and goosebumps skittered across her skin at the sound. Besides his good looks, she had once loved his deep, raspy voice that was as seductive as his smile and dimples.

"For almost thirteen years, I honored your request to stay away from you, but Cree, I can't any longer. I want you back in my life in any capacity I can get you."

"Why?" she asked.

She couldn't for the life of her understand why he'd come to her, knowing how she felt about him. Sure, she cared about his well-being. She wasn't totally heartless, but she had her limits and already knew working with Tristan would push every single one of them.

Tristan slid along the edge of the desk and didn't stop until their legs were touching.

"Because I owe you," he said. "You should've always been my agent because, in my heart, I knew one day you'd be the best in the industry. I was young and..." He shrugged his broad shoulders that looked as if they were going to burst through his suit jacket. "Basically, I made the wrong decision. More importantly, I've missed you."

Cree wasn't sure how to respond. So she said nothing, but when he reached forward and cupped her cheek, bringing his handsome face within inches of hers, she wanted to push him away. She couldn't. She might've wanted him out of her face, but more than that, she wanted to brush her lips over his. Just one little...

"I want you back in my life, Cree," Tristan said, his voice thick with emotion as he stared into her eyes. "I want my wife back."

Chapter Six

Tristan regretted those last five words the moment they left his mouth. He wanted to punch himself when Cree froze, then jerked away from his touch as if she'd been burned.

"*Ex-wife*, and you'll never have me again!" she snapped and rolled her chair back from the desk before bolting out of her seat.

Tristan stood also and moved from around the desk, keeping a little distance between them as they stood in the middle of the office floor.

"If I were to take you on as a client, and that's a *huge* if, there'd be nothing between us except a professional relationship." Anger dripped from each word as Cree glared at him. "Right now, though, I'm still unsure of whether adding you to my client roster is worth it. Yes, financially it would be, but doing so would be a bad idea. Because this... *us*"—she waved a hand back and forth between them—"will never happen again. So if that's why you're here under the disguise of needing representation, you can forget it."

"Okay." Tristan lifted his hands out in front of him in hopes of getting her to settle down. He had to talk fast. Cree would probably only give him a few more minutes of her time, and he had to make them count.

He played his hand too quickly by mentioning he wanted his wife back. He also shouldn't have said anything about missing her, even if it was true. The only excuse he could come up with for why he'd run off at the mouth was that being in her presence again was screwing with his mind... and his heart. Whether she wanted to or not, she would always hold a special spot in his heart, and in all the years they'd been apart, that hadn't changed.

He'd been twenty-one when they'd secretly eloped. Not even their parents knew, thanks to Cree. Only his brother, Quincy and her sister, Essence, were aware of their nuptials. Cree had wanted to keep it quiet, especially from anyone in the business, until she had acquired a few more clients for her sports agency.

In hindsight, they'd been way too young to get married even though he'd been crazy in love with her. They had tied the knot three days before their relationship imploded with the news about him landing a new agent.

God, he would never forget that night. He'd known Cree would be upset, but he had underestimated just how furious she'd be. He soon found out when she kicked him out of her apartment and served him with divorce papers shortly after he had signed with Philadelphia. He'd been shocked she hadn't tried to get half of what he stood to make from the NFL team. Instead, all she wanted was out of the marriage.

He had refused to sign the divorce papers. For months, he begged her for forgiveness and another chance—offering her anything she wanted. He loved her too much to let her go without a fight, but then she'd showed up at his condo in Philly.

He thought she was coming back to him, but instead, she told him, if he really loved her, he'd let her go.

He did, and to this day, that had been the biggest mistake of his life.

"I'm here in a professional capacity because I need to make some decisions about those offers, and I need to make them soon," he said, pointing at the documents spread out on her desk. "I need your help with that, and I want you to represent me. Please, Cree. Don't let your anger toward me make you and your agency miss out on millions of dollars."

Appealing to her business sense was the way to go now. She might want to maintain a hard *no* where he was concerned, but she knew how much money he could generate for their firm. He was counting on that side of her to make the right decision.

And then there was Warren. If this could help with whatever was going on with...

"If my firm represents you..."

Excitement raced through him as she laid out her demands, including taking a higher percentage than most agents took. He didn't care. This was just the beginning of a plan to have her back in his life again, and when that happened, he was never letting her go.

"I'll read through the offers this evening. In the meantime, set up an appointment with Shantel on your way out. There'll be a contract here tomorrow afternoon for you to sign with us. I'll represent you, but Tristan, don't make me regret this."

"I won't, and for the record, I'm only interested in the offers that'll keep me in Chicago. I'm here to stay, Cree." He looked at her pointedly. Soon, she'd find out just how serious he was regarding them picking up where they left off years ago. "I'd also consider offers which might require some travel, but nothing that will keep me away for more than three days at a time."

She maintained eye contact as she slowly nodded. "Understood."

But did she really understand? Did she have any idea that he planned to fight for her, and he wasn't above fighting dirty? If she didn't, she'd find out soon enough.

A knock sounded on her office door.

"Come in," Cree said.

A tall, dark skin brother strolled into the room. He was a big guy, looking as if he'd probably played football or basketball at some point in his life.

Recognition had shown on the man's face when they made eye contact, but he didn't acknowledge Tristan. Instead, he gave Cree his full attention. His gaze skimmed her body and the way he'd done it didn't look professional.

Tension coiled inside of Tristan. The one thing he didn't know was whether Cree had a man. He hoped not. If she wasn't married, there'd be nothing to stop him from pursuing her.

"Sorry to interrupt, Cree, but Shantel wasn't at her desk. Should I come back later?" the man asked, barely sparing Tristan another glance.

"No, I'm glad you're here, Milton. Come on in. Mr. Whitmore was just leaving."

Well, damn. Tristan might've been planning on leaving soon, but she didn't have to dismiss him so carelessly.

Cree returned her attention to him. "Mr. Whitmore, I'll be in touch tomorrow. Have a good evening."

Tristan approached her. "Oh, so we're back to Mr. Whitmore?" he said, briefly placing a hand on her waist as he started to pass her, and he didn't miss the way she shivered. "See you soon." He walked out without a backwards glance.

Soon. Soon he'd have her again.

* * *

"Wow, Tristan Whitmore, huh?" Milton Banks, the firm's private investigator said as he took a seat in front of Cree's desk. "Seems you're moving up in the world, and my guess is your client list just got more interesting."

Cree chuckled and sat across from him, realizing Tristan's documents were still on her desk. She made quick work of putting everything back into the large envelope. Milton knew a lot about their clients, but for some reason, she didn't want him to know any more than necessary about Tristan.

And interesting? That was a good word for Tristan, but she didn't want to talk about him. Especially since her heart was still beating faster than it should be. Now that he was gone, maybe she could settle down and forget he'd ever been there. But that was going to be impossible since she could still smell his cologne.

"Just another day at the office," she said noncommittally. "I hope you have some good news for me. What did you find out about Andrea? Is she staying out of trouble like she agreed to?" Cree asked of one of their clients. She was on the verge of cutting the B-list actress from her roster because of all the negative attention she'd been garnering over the years. Lately, she stayed in the tabloids with one scandal after another.

"I'll have a formal report to you by the end of the day. In the meantime, I'll let you decide if she's keeping her agreement," Milton said and handed Cree his high-end camera.

Cree sighed at the first photo, then started skimming through the others. Andrea definitely liked getting naked. Too bad she didn't care where she did it. She and the man she was having sex with appeared to be in an alley.

It always amazed Cree of the photos and videos Milton could get without anyone knowing they were being watched. Then again, even if Andrea had known he was filming her, she probably wouldn't have cared. The woman had been a problem to work with from day one. But Cree thought the movie and a commercial deal Andrea had gotten recently would make her think twice before doing anything that could cause her to lose the deals. Apparently not.

"This girl has no decorum."

"Yeah, she is a lot. My guess is, with some of her antics but not this particular one, she's trying to stay relevant. Maybe thinking any press is good press. Not sure what she was thinking in this situation. They could've gone back to her place for their rendezvous," Milton said.

The former Chicago P.D. detective had been working for their law firm for over five years and had become invaluable to Cree and the partners.

She handed him back the camera. "It would be good if she could stay relevant by doing something that shows her in a good light. Maybe volunteer work like I suggested last week. At least she didn't get arrested this time for indecent exposure. I think our PR department is frustrated. They had a hard time spinning a tale regarding her buying weed and some pills from a known drug dealer last month. Who's the man in those photos?"

"A local DJ. I haven't seen the two of them together before. So, I'm assuming he's the new guy since Grant dumped her."

Grant, an A-list actor, had been a mentor of sorts to Andrea. That was until she'd gotten arrested recently. Not wanting his reputation to take a hit, he had dumped her and had done it very publicly. Cree was fairly sure the scene had been planned by Grant's people.

47

At any rate, she needed to decide what to do about the woman. She'd bring it up at the next staff meeting.

Milton shoved the camera back into his bag. "So, are congratulations on signing Tristan Whitmore in order? Rumor has it that he's going to be a hot commodity even though he's no longer playing football. I heard a couple of NFL teams are looking at him for coaching positions."

Cree was always impressed at how in-the-know Milton always seemed to be.

"Yeah, the league loves him," Cree said, still not wanting to discuss her ex.

The only time she talked about clients with Milton was if she needed information on them. Tristan's life, for the most part, had played out in the media, especially for the past few months. From what she knew so far, she didn't need Milton's assistance. No, any research into Tristan would be done by her. Which probably wasn't the best idea, but for now, she'd keep details about him as a client in-house.

"What about you?" Milton asked, and Cree glanced at him.

"What about me?"

Milton was a handsome guy with tawny brown skin, friendly eyes, and a roguish smile. Though he had shown interest in more than a professional way, she never encouraged him.

"I mean what do you think of Whitmore as a potential client?" Milton watched her carefully, and she wondered if he knew something about Tristan that she should know.

"This is not public information, but he's looking for representation."

Milton nodded, still watching her as if he knew something but was debating on saying it. "I see. Well, based on the interaction earlier, he seems to have taken a liking to you."

Cree chuckled and waved him off. "I think it's safe to say he's a flirt, which doesn't faze me. I don't mix business with pleasure." She'd done that once with Tristan, and she wouldn't do it again.

A slow smile kicked up the corners of Milton's mouth. "So you've told me, more than once. With that said, though, if you're almost done here, how about dinner at Alla Vita?" he asked casually, but Cree didn't miss the hope in his eyes.

They'd gone out together a few times over the years, but lately, it hadn't felt like they were going out as friends or coworkers. Something had changed on Milton's part. Cree recognized the signs of a man who's interested in more than just friendship, and she'd made it clear they could only ever be friends. She just wasn't sure he got the message.

"I'm going to have to pass." She glanced at her watch. "I have a meeting this evening. As a matter of fact, I have a few things I need to take care of before then. Is there anything else we need to discuss regarding Andrea?"

Milton snorted and glanced down at his camera bag before looking at her again, then stood. "Right. Business," he said and chuckled. "Got it."

Good, she thought, because she didn't want things to get weird between them. He was a great investigator who they'd come to rely on.

"Maybe some other time. As friends of course," Milton said. "I have a question for you, though. If Tristan Whitmore would've asked you out for dinner tonight, would you have said yes?"

"*Hell* no," she said emphatically. "I told you that I don't mix business with pleasure. And if we sign Whitmore, it will be all business."

She proclaimed the words with such force Cree wasn't sure

if she was trying to convince Milton or herself. Either way, she couldn't mess this up by letting her attraction to Tristan screw with her mind, heart, or her job.

Not this time. Not ever again.

Chapter Seven

"What do you mean you're selling the house?" Bethany screeched the moment she stepped into the kitchen where part of the family was congregated. Her piercing cry of anger echoed through the huge space, and Tristan cringed.

He'd known his sister would have issues with his announcement, but he was ready for her. He was done carrying her financially, and selling some property was just the beginning of the changes he was making for his future.

He sipped his steaming hot coffee as he stared at his sister. At thirty-years-old, Bethany was the baby of the family and could best be described as spoiled, selfish, entitled, and sometimes demanding. Tristan hated that he played a role in her turning out the way she had. Almost five years older, he had always been the protective big brother and made sure she wanted for nothing.

But she was a grown woman now, and his priorities had shifted. Of course, he'd always be there for his family, but there were going to be some changes.

"Where are we supposed to live?" Bethany snapped, standing between her parents who were seated at the large kitchen table.

Though it was early Sunday morning, she looked like she'd been awake for hours. Or maybe she was just getting home. He wasn't sure. With the size of the house, it was hard keeping track of who was home or not.

Either way, she looked pulled together considering the time of day. Her dreadlocks were piled on top of her head in a stylish twist, and her face was perfectly made up like usual. Wearing a designer sweater, skin-tight jeans, and thigh-high boots she could be going anywhere.

Their grandfather, who also lived in the house, was shaking his head. He loved his grandchildren, but he often said the family, including him, created a monster when it came to Bethany.

"You're going to live in your own house or apartment that *you* pay for," Tristan's dad said before Tristan could respond. "There is no reason why you should expect your brother to continue supporting your extravagant lifestyle."

"He doesn't pay for everything where I'm concerned," his sister countered weakly. "But that's beside the point, Dad. If he sells the family home, where are you guys going to live? Is Tristan throwing you out, knowing you can't afford a place like this?"

She turned her angry gaze back on Tristan, and he snorted. Damn, he was getting sick of the women in his life glaring at him. First, Cree the other day, and now Bethany. At least with Cree, he deserved her anger. Thankfully he had smoothed things over with her and was now signed with *Ellis, Priestly, and Watts Law Firm.*

Two days ago, he had gone back to Cree's office and made it official by signing a contract. Of course, he had to endure another speech from her insisting they would only have a professional relationship. And of course, he agreed to keep the peace, but in his mind, his plan was working. He was back in her life, and it was only a matter of time before she realized she was still in love with him, like he was in love with her.

"Tristan, are you even listening?" Bethany said, her voice louder than before. She pointed an accusatory finger at him. "I bet this sudden change has something to do with a woman. Who is she? Is she forcing you to disown your family so you'll have more money to spend on her? Or is she withholding..."

"Beth!" their mother snapped. "That's enough! And we're sitting right here. Use your inside voice and stop acting like a child."

Tristan was impressed his sister had part of that right. Yes, he was making changes because of a woman but not the way Bethany was implying. He would never turn his back on his family, but he wanted his life in order because he was ready for marriage and a family of his own. Granted, it was presumptuous of him to think he'd get a second chance with Cree, but he had to try. He couldn't imagine his future without her in it.

So while trying to win her back, he was getting his house in order, in a manner of speaking. For the most part, his family members were self-sufficient except for the properties. He wanted to make sure they all had their own homes, in their names, so they didn't rely on him as much. Especially his sister.

Bethany huffed out a breath. "How am I supposed to react when you're springing this on us out of nowhere?" she said to Tristan. "I can't just snap my fingers and have all my stuff moved out."

"Yeah, actually, you can," he countered. "Money talks and you have it. Or at least you should."

"Besides, it's not out of nowhere," their grandfather added.

"Tristan has been talking about this for a while. Apparently, you weren't taking him seriously."

His mother's father was in his early eighties and was as mentally sharp as someone half his age. His salt and pepper hair was cut low, and he was dressed in a black tracksuit, looking healthier than Tristan had ever seen him.

"Or he's only talked about it when I'm in Philadelphia," Bethany countered and stomped over to the refrigerator in her high-heel boots.

"That reminds me," Tristan said. "I'm also planning to put the Philly condo up for sale at the end of the month. So, I suggest you move your stuff out of there too."

Bethany had just grabbed orange juice from the refrigerator and whirled around to face him. "Seriously, Tristan?" she yelled and slammed the bottle on the counter with a thud. "That's in less than three weeks! You could've given me more notice."

"You're right. I probably should've told you that, since I've retired and have moved back to Chicago, I'm selling the properties in Philly. Everything in the condo is mine. So, moving the few clothes and personal items you have there shouldn't take much."

He loved his family, and more than anything, he enjoyed giving them the type of life all of them had dreamed of. His parents and grandfather, as well as Quincy, had never asked for much. Still, a year after joining the NFL, Tristan had purchased the family house, a huge, eight-bedroom, ten-bathroom, nine-thousand square foot home in Hinsdale, a suburb of Chicago. The place was large enough for all of them to live comfortably without feeling like they were on top of each other.

This was something they'd talked about for years prior to him entering the NFL. So when the home was purchased, they all moved in. Though Tristan only lived there occasionally during the off season, it always felt like home. As for the condo in Philly, he lived there those first couple of years. But when they started the nonprofit and hired Bethany, she split her time between Chicago and Philadelphia. Tristan let her move into the two-bedroom condo, and he purchased a house for himself.

"So where is everyone going?" Bethany asked in a calmer tone though she was still glaring at him.

"We're getting a smaller place. Something more manageable," their mother said. "For years I've said we don't need all this space, especially since you kids are rarely here. And none of you have blessed us with grandchildren," she added with a pointed look at each of them, which they both ignored. "Three or four bedrooms is enough for me, your father, and Papa."

Instead of staying at the family house, Tristan was currently renting a luxury apartment. He loved his privacy, and though he had his own space at the big house, it wasn't the same. When he moved back to Chicago, he had needed time and solitude to figure out how to embrace his new reality. He was only thirty-four and hadn't planned on retiring this soon. He'd still been dealing with the shock of his world turning upside down.

But now he had a plan. While winning Cree back, he wanted to have his own space for them to get to know each other again.

The real estate agent he contracted with would be working to find something for him, as well as his parents. Quincy had only lived in the family house for a year before buying his own place. That left Bethany, who he already knew would try to stall.

"I suggest you start looking for a place," Tristan said and stood.

"With what money?" his sister grumbled.

"Young lady, you need to fix your attitude," their father

ground out as he stood to his six-two height. "Your brother has set you up financially with a job at the nonprofit and money in the bank. Surely, you didn't think you'd be mooching off him for the rest of your life, did you?"

By the expression on her face, she had. Unbelievable. Not only did she have a great paying job doing fundraising for Tristan's nonprofit, but he'd set up a trust fund for her. She'd had access to it since she was twenty-five, and it was enough to live comfortably for the rest of her life. That is, if she didn't spend it all on clothes, shoes and other accessories.

"Spoiled brat," Tristan mumbled.

He started out of the room but slowed and glanced over his shoulder. "Bethany, you either get with the program or you're going to find all your designer crap out on the front lawn when these houses sell."

She gasped. "You wouldn't."

"Try me."

He sauntered out of the room thinking about the next step in his *Win-Cree-Back* plan. He had Cree, *the lawyer,* back in his life. Now he just needed Cree, *the woman,* back.

Chapter Eight

Cree jotted down a few notes regarding Tristan's endorsement offers that she wanted to discuss with him. She planned to suggest he request more money for one of them since they wanted to shoot three commercials within two weeks in Atlanta. Either way, she wasn't sure he'd agree to it since he'd been adamant about not traveling much.

She sat back and rocked in her chair, wondering why he was so against traveling, especially with the money they were offering. Of course, her first thought was that he had a woman here in Chicago who he didn't want to be away from for long. However, Cree nixed that idea. One thing she knew about Tristan was that he was a one-woman man. She was sure that hadn't changed. No way he'd touch her or flirt with her the way he had the other day if there was someone else in his life.

He wasn't that guy, and Cree would bet her life savings on that.

"And why am I even thinking about this?" she mumbled to herself, frustrated with the way her thoughts had gone.

The worst part about that was she really wanted to know,

but why? Why did she even care? When he came in to sign the contract, she'd made it clear the two of them working together again would be strictly business. It had to be that way. She couldn't fall for his handsome face or the nostalgia of him being back in her life again.

But what if she...

A knock sounded on her office door, and Cree wanted to scream *thank you for saving me from myself* to whoever it was.

"Come in," she called out, and the door swung open. She tried not to let her disappointment show when her visitor appeared. She would've preferred anyone but him. "Hey, Warren."

"Hi, gotta a minute?" he asked, and Cree closed the file that held Tristan's information.

In his early sixties, Warren's pale face was showing a hint of wrinkles, but he still had a head of salt and pepper hair. Considering his workload and long days, his gray eyes were as sharp as the day he'd hired her around ten years ago.

She'd been excited to join his firm, one of the top law offices in the city. For the most part, her experience had been good, especially since she'd been able to make partner sooner than she'd expected. But lately she'd been antsy, and a lot of that had to do with him trying to micromanage her. It hadn't always been that way. Not until recently.

"Congratulations on signing, Tristan Whitmore," he said and unbuttoned his suit jacket before sitting down. "I didn't realize you were scouting him. When did that happen?" he asked the question casually, but Cree wondered if there was something more behind it. She no longer trusted him, and she wasn't a hundred percent sure why. Just a gut feeling.

Slow to respond, she debated on what to tell him.

"You're acting as if I don't usually bring in high-profile clients," she finally said and rocked back in her chair. "I brought in several this year and have clocked more billable hours than any other partner. So, what's really going on here?"

Warren sighed. "I'm just asking and making conversation. Why are you getting defensive?"

"Because it doesn't feel like just conversation. It feels as if you're fishing for something. If there's something you want to know, just ask."

"I want to know the relationship between you and Whitmore. There was definitely tension between the two of you when I introduced myself to him the other day. If there's a problem, I can assist with representing him."

Ha! She just bet he could. As a huge sports fan, he'd kill for a client like Tristan.

"That won't be necessary. I was his agent before he signed on with Ralph Dawson. You probably showed up when I was asking why Dawson was now his former agent."

"So, Whitmore came looking for you? Not the other way around?"

"Correct," Cree said simply. No need sharing more information than necessary.

"Interesting."

"Why is that interesting?"

Warren looked at her as if she should know. "No offense or anything, but I'm surprised Whitmore would leave Dawson and then ask *you* to represent him. Dawson is the best in his field. It's just interesting is all."

Cree couldn't be mad at his word choice because she'd thought it interesting too... at first. Now she believed Tristan truly was trying to make things right between them professionally. Though she still thought he had a secret agenda. Specifically, for them to get back together, but she took him at his word when he told her he wanted her to represent him because he owed her.

He didn't owe her, but she didn't tell him that. Like he had mentioned, they'd been so young back then, and she'd been all in her feelings with the way he had signed with another agent. But Cree truly did understand his reasoning. Had she been him, she probably would've signed with Ralph Dawson too. The man had an incredible track record.

"Full disclosure," she said. "Tristan was one of my clients when I first opened my sports agency years ago. I haven't had much interaction with him since he switched agencies shortly before his second year in the league."

Warren nodded. "And why did he leave your agency in the first place?"

Cree watched him carefully, wondering if he already knew the answer and was waiting to see if she'd be straight with him. Or if he genuinely didn't know. She couldn't tell, which was no surprise. Like most attorneys, he wasn't easy to read.

"You said yourself Dawson is the best. I had only been an agent for a year or so, and Whitmore felt, with Ralph Dawson's track record, he could get him a larger contract." She shrugged. "And I couldn't much blame him. Even back then, Ralph was known for getting his clients record-breaking deals."

"So, Whitmore wasn't loyal to you. He jumped ship at the first chance he got to sign with a bigger fish, so to speak."

Cree schooled her features. When he phrased it like that, the memory of that time in her life reared its wicked head. So maybe it was still a bit of a sore subject for her. But she was determined to get over it and leave the past in the past.

But it was more than that. Her previous relationship with Tristan was complicated. They'd been friends and then lovers before he had become her client, and that made their professional relationship tough. It wasn't always easy to separate the personal from the business, even more so after marrying him.

"Why do you think he left Dawson's agency to sign with us?"

"According to him, he felt he owed me for getting his career started, and he wanted a chance to work with me in this new stage of his life."

Warren nodded again. "Is that why he only signed a nine-month contract? Seems a bit odd."

She could be honest and tell him that she had suggested the short terms. She could tell him it was a test for them both to see if they could work together. Or she could keep the reason to herself.

Warren didn't have to know the *why*, and there was no reason for him to be questioning her like this unless he was fishing for information. What type of information she wasn't sure. Maybe he sensed she was thinking about leaving and starting her own firm.

"That's what the client wanted," she said, stretching the truth.

If Warren followed up with Tristan, she already knew her ex would say something similar. Then he'd tell her about the conversation. Even if they hadn't been in touch in years, Cree already knew Tristan was protective of her. Always had been, which was something she had loved about him. Despite knowing she could take care of herself, he'd always been willing and ready to come to her defense.

The other day, he had sensed the tension between her and Warren and had questioned her about him. If he had picked up on it in the few minutes he had spent with the guy, then Warren's behavior lately wasn't just her imagination.

"He has some impressive endorsement offers that will make this firm an obscene amount of money." She shrugged like it wasn't a big deal, when in fact it was a huge deal. The money she and the firm would make off those deals was incredible. "I would think the bottom line would be what's most important to you right now. So why all the questions?"

Before Warren could respond, someone knocked on the door. Cree really didn't care about whatever he was going to say, and this interruption couldn't have come at a better time.

"Come in," she called out and stood just as Shantel entered with a large paper bag.

She lifted it up by the handles, a twinkle in her eyes as she said, "Your lunch just arrived."

Cree hadn't ordered lunch. Yet this was just the distraction she needed.

"Oh good. Right on time," she said, wondering if there was really something in the bag. It didn't matter. She was going to make sure Shantel got a big, fat bonus this year.

The woman was a godsend and always came through for Cree when she least expected. It was easy to forget Shantel didn't work just for her. She worked for all the partners. She was so efficient in everything she did and always predicted what Cree needed or wanted before being asked. She'd been with the firm for almost eight years, and right now, she was Cree's favorite person.

"Warren, I assume we're done here," Cree said when he didn't move.

"Yes, I guess we are." He eventually stood and moved around Shantel toward the door. "Keep me posted regarding Whitmore."

Cree folded her arms across her chest and frowned. "Why? I don't usually have to report to you regarding *my* clients. Why now?"

"Because he's now one of our most high-profile clients, and I want to make sure he's treated right. When other athletes realize he's acquired our services, they might follow. So don't mess this up."

Anger boiled inside of Cree. Normally, their private conversations stayed behind closed doors where their support staff couldn't hear, but since he started it...

"First of all, I'm a partner here too, and I know how to take care of my clients, high-profile or not. Which is why they come to me. They know how good I am at my job," she snapped. If his flinching at her tone was any indication, her words came out harsher than she intended. "I don't know what this is all about, Warren—you coming in here questioning me—but understand, I've been at this a long time, and I know what I'm doing. Enjoy the rest of your day," she said dismissively and turned her attention to Shantel.

Warren stormed out without another word, and Cree took several deep breaths to gather herself. She was going to have to watch her back with that guy.

"Thanks for the save," Cree said quietly to Shantel. "Sorry you had to hear all that."

"No problem, and just so you know, anything I heard stays right here."

"I appreciate that, and..." Before Cree could continue, the scent of bacon, garlic and other delicious spices met her nose as Shantel handed her the bag. "Wait, you really did order me lunch?"

What surprised Cree more when she peeked into the bag was the meal had come from her favorite Puerto Rican restaurant. There were two jibarito sandwiches inside. These weren't just any sandwiches. These were jibarito plantain burgers.

"Oh my goodness, I could kiss you right now!" Cree practically squealed. She hadn't had one in months, maybe even a year.

Fried green plantains were used instead of bread, and the sandwich contained a couple of beef patties, glazed bacon, cheese, tomatoes, lettuce, and a garlicky mayo that was to die for.

"Umm, I didn't order the lunch," Shantel said, a huge grin on her face as she pulled a note from behind her back. "But I was given strict instructions to make sure you got it, and my favorite part is you have to share it with me." She laughed and handed Cree the card. "So one of those sandwiches is mine, and by your reaction, I can't wait to eat it."

Cree skimmed the card and almost whimpered at the words in Tristan's handwriting.

If I know you, you probably skip more lunches than you eat. Here's a little something for you and Shantel because, if she has to put up with you every day, I'm sure she deserves a free meal.

Cree couldn't help but laugh. "That man," she murmured.

Shantel glanced at the open door, then back at Cree before whispering, "I knew there was history between you two. Care to share?"

Cree shook her head while still smiling. "It's complicated."

"Ahh, understood. Well, I'll just take my sandwich and go, but if you talk to Mr. Complicated, please tell him I said thanks and to feel free to send us lunch anytime."

Cree laughed again. "Will do."

She closed the door behind Shantel and didn't waste any time digging into her meal. Not only was she hungry, but the jibarito was as good as she remembered. She thought about calling Tristan to thank him, but he was scheduled to come by the office in a couple of hours to go over his offers. She'd thank him then.

God, she missed his thoughtfulness. Heck, if she was honest with herself, Cree missed everything about the man. Which meant she was going to have to work extra hard to keep their meetings professional. Her self-control when it came to him was no match for his determination when he wanted something. And he had made it clear, in so many words, that he wanted her.

But she could be just as stubborn because there was no way they could go back to what they once shared. Especially with her representing him. Even if deep down inside she wanted to get reacquainted with his alluring body.

"I can't. I won't, and I'll just keep telling myself that," she mumbled and took another bite of her sandwich and groaned. "Oh, this is so good."

Still, she couldn't let this kind gesture make her lose herself to Tristan again. He might be good at getting what he wanted, but she was strong enough to resist him.

Chapter Nine

"I'm going to kill him," Cree mumbled as she drove through downtown Chicago at the peak of after-work rush hour. It had already been a long day, and sitting in bumper-to-bumper traffic was making her madder at Tristan for changing the plans.

When he called a short while ago, she'd thanked him for lunch but then wondered why he was calling when he should've been there. He'd been scheduled to come to her office to go over his endorsement offers but had called, talking fast, while telling her he couldn't make it. He had suggested rescheduling, but then he'd come up with the idea of her coming to him.

At first Cree had shot the idea down. When it came to him, and the fear she'd have no self-control where he was concerned, she preferred to meet in her office. There, she could be professional without worrying about being tempted to kiss him or something equally stupid.

Yeah, she could admit—she had a problem. Since lunch, he'd been all she could think about, and that was a problem because in the past, the man had been irresistible. Now? He was equally irresistible but even more so since she'd sworn to keep her guard up around him. She'd gone years without thinking about him every minute of the day, and all that self-control was shot to hell.

"Ugh, I can't stand him."

She hated feeling like this. She should've just insisted they reschedule, and then she wouldn't be in this position. But no, she went along with his stupid idea of meeting him at a condo he was touring this evening and then they'd talk.

Supposedly, he was in the process of house hunting. His real estate agent found a place that she insisted he had to see now, the same time he was supposed to meet with Cree. There were several offers on the place, but if he liked it enough, the seller's agent would give him until tonight to submit an offer.

"His butt better not be lying," Cree mumbled as she turned left and started looking for the address. There were several high-rises in the area, one as jaw-dropping impressive as the next.

Tristan was lucky she was curious about the condo he wanted to see. There'd been a time when she had considered buying in the area, but these were way out of her budget. Her sister, Dorian's fiancé, Lynix, owned a penthouse not too far from here. His place was gorgeous with great views. She had a feeling that this place would be even more awe-inspiring.

Just as she pulled into the circular drive of the condominium complex, Tristan walked outside. He pointed to a small area several feet away for her to park. As she followed where he'd pointed, she stole a few glances at him in her rearview mirror. His swagger was on point, and she had to stop herself from smiling. Gone was the young kid who'd had no money, no life experience, and no idea what he'd do if he didn't play professional football. But he had confidence in himself, big dreams, and a ton of talent.

Now look at him. Tristan Whitmore was all man and had accomplished everything he had set out to do. Cree couldn't help but be proud and impressed by him.

She backed into a parking spot, then watched him through her windshield. "*Ooo wee*. How the heck does he just keep getting sexier?"

Tristan had gotten his hair cut since the last time she'd seen him, and his face was clean-shaven like usual. Again, with the bling. That was one thing Cree didn't remember about him— his love for jewelry. But maybe when you made more money than you could possibly spend in a lifetime, you had to find something to spend it on. Diamonds and silver appeared to be his choice.

Cree liked the look on him, though. It added to his bad-boy swagger. Large diamond studs sparkled in his ears, a thick silver chain peeked out from the collar of his short-sleeved T-shirt, and a platinum watch and chain-link bracelet graced his wrists.

Her gaze quickly took in his powerful-looking body, admiring the way his gray T-shirt left nothing to the imagination. Big, broad shoulders, a chest that showcased muscular pecs, and his sinewy biceps that were bursting from the short sleeves had her moaning.

Hmm... more tattoos.

Both of his muscular arms had a sleeve of elaborate tattoos. Definitely more than he used to have. She wondered how much of his body was covered with them now. Then again, she didn't want to know because she wasn't interested. She just had to keep reminding herself of that.

I'm not interested. Really, I'm not.

"Hey. You made it," Tristan said, opening the driver's side door for her.

He helped her out of the car, and when their hands touched, the tingle scurrying through her body had her shivering.

Yeah, it was not good that her body was so in tuned to him like this. Especially when his alluring bedroom eyes met hers, and a slow smile kicked up the corners of his gorgeous lips. And then those damn dimples made an appearance.

This was ridiculous. She should still be pissed at him, but it's like her girlie parts didn't get that memo. Just a look and he had her licking her lips and squeezing her thighs together. Clearly, she'd gone too long without a man, and her body was betraying her.

The man was too fine for his own good, and he was too much temptation.

She huffed out a breath, frustrated with herself.

"I know you're mad at me," Tristan said, misinterpreting her frustrated sigh.

Still holding her hand, he gave it a little tug, pulling Cree against his hard body, and she was defenseless to fight him. Instead of fighting him or herself, she melted into him, loving the way his strong, powerful arms held her close.

She had always been attracted to tall men, and Tristan had several inches on her even in her heels. And as he held her close and tightly, she slid her arms around his waist. She breathed in his woodsy scent that had a hint of citrus and marveled at how perfect this moment felt.

A little too perfect.

Being held by him was like snuggling under a cashmere blanket on a cold winter's night. It felt like she was exactly where she was supposed to be. Wrapped in his arms. Soaking up his strength. And being still... even for a moment.

She'd been working so much lately, Cree couldn't remember the last time she'd been in a man's arms. Even still, no one had ever held her the way Tristan did, and she didn't realize how much she had needed to be held. Didn't realize she needed to feel cherished in a way that only he could do.

Yeah, this was definitely a little too perfect.

If a friendly hug could get her mentally and emotionally twisted up inside, she was in more trouble than she realized when it came to Tristan.

He gave her a tight squeeze and placed a lingering kiss on the side of her forehead before releasing her. When he did, Cree hoped he didn't apologize for hugging her. Maybe if she didn't make a big deal about it, he wouldn't either.

Since he had come back into her life, she'd given him a hard time—wanting him to stay away from her unless they were discussing business. Something within her had just shifted, and she didn't want to think on it too much.

"You look amazing," he said, snapping her out of her thoughts.

"Thank you." She reached into the vehicle and grabbed her laptop bag. "Now why am I here?"

He placed a hand at the small of her back and guided her to the grand entrance of the building.

"You being here kept me from having to postpone our meeting, and I'm sorry about that, but thanks for coming. I know you're pissed I had to change the plans, but I really wanted to see this place before it was too late. I promise, once I check out this condo, I'll look over whatever you want me to and sign whatever needs to be signed. I figured this was better than me rescheduling for a later date."

Cree nodded. "Okay."

Tristan slowed and frowned down at her. "Okay? That's it? You're not going to give me hell for having you come out here? Are you feeling okay?"

She laughed. "No, I'm not going to give you a hard time, but I can if it'll make you feel better."

"Oh, no. That's alright," he said quickly. "Let's go before you change your mind. I'm told this place is a must see."

A few minutes later, they stepped off the elevator and into a place that stole Cree's breath. The first thing she saw was a wall of floor to ceiling windows, and she crossed the room to them as if being pulled by a magnet.

"Wow," was all she could say as she stood in front of the windows. The condo was so high up, most of the view of Lake Michigan was unobstructed and what a view.

"Wow indeed," Tristan said from beside her.

"Oh, you made it." A high-pitched voice sounded from behind them along with the clicking of high heels on the hardwood floors.

They turned from the window as a woman, looking to be in her mid-forties, dressed in a beautiful tan pantsuit with matching heels, approached. Her wide, genuine smile greeted them before she stretched out her hand.

"Good to see you two."

"Hey, Cathy. Good to see you also," Tristan said, shaking her hand and then placing his hand on Cree's back. "This is a friend of mine, Cree Priestly."

"Pleasure to meet you, Cree." They shook hands before Cathy turned back to the unit and spread her arms wide. "So, what are your first impressions?"

"It's bigger than I expected and impressive," Tristan said as he roamed around.

Cree had been so busy looking out the windows, she hadn't even noticed the rooms. The condo was a corner unit, and the open floor plan looked to have been decorated by an interior designer. The contemporary decor was airy and had clean lines and a minimalist vibe. It appeared a little cold, but no less exquisite.

As her gaze scanned the large space, she noted that, though the kitchen and dining area had partial lake views, the rooms mainly overlooked the skyline.

"Cree, I'm not sure if Tristan mentioned, but this is a three-bedroom, four-bathroom unit with rooftop access. It's the last available unit in the building and already has multiple offers."

Okay, so Tristan had been telling her the truth.

The agent started her spiel, giving them a little history on the new construction, expressing it was the best of downtown and lake front living. While they strolled from one room to another, Cathy not only talked about the space, but also the building's amenities. Based on the extensive list, the HOA fee was probably an arm and a leg.

"The luxurious amenities have been designed to meet your convenience, as well as your wellness needs. Once we're done up here, I'll show you everything the building has to offer."

The secondary bedrooms weren't huge, but what they lacked in space, they made up in views. What she didn't like was that one bedroom's view was of another condominium.

She had once thought living downtown would be fun and convenient, but the idea of someone being able to see into the bedroom didn't appeal to her. But when they reached the master suite, all thoughts of anyone looking in flew from her brain. It had the same lake view as the living room, and it was breathtaking.

"This would be the selling point for me," Tristan said as if reading her mind. "It's a nice size, and I like the idea of *not* looking into someone else's bedroom."

Cree wondered if he was seriously thinking about buying the place. So far, the real estate agent hadn't mentioned the price, but Cree assumed she had already discussed it with Tristan.

When Cathy's phone rang, she excused herself while they checked out the humongous bathroom and walk-in closet. Both separately were the size of the secondary bedrooms.

"You're right, this space would be the selling point," Cree mumbled as she took in the two-person soaking tub that sat in front of a huge window with exquisite views.

The window might be a turn off, unless the glass was one-way glass, where they could see out but no one could see in. Still, she'd kill for a bathroom like this one. Then again, she would never get any work done because she'd never leave the space.

"So, you like the place?" Tristan asked. He was casually leaning against the doorjamb looking at her.

Never one for holding in her opinion, she said, "It's beautiful. The views alone are probably worth every penny of the sale price. It has a lot of square footage, but why would you need all this space? Unless..."

"I'm not married, and I'm not seeing anyone," he said quickly. "But that won't always be the case. I want a place that's big enough for the family I hope to one day have."

Cree's chest tightened at hearing him talking about having a family. She tried not to react and kept her face neutral, but she wasn't sure if it was working. When they got married, she had vowed to be with him until death. Yet, at the first sign of trouble, she cut him loose. Thinking about that had her feeling sick. Her mother often said she was too impulsive. That had been a prime example.

Shaking the thought free, she said, "What do you think of the place? Can you see yourself living here?"

He glanced around the bathroom and then pushed away

from the doorjamb and gazed into the bedroom. "I don't know. Maybe," he finally said and turned back to her. "Could you?"

"It doesn't matter if I can or can't," she hurried to say, making sure he didn't get any ideas, assuming he didn't already have ideas. "You're the one who'll be living here."

After a slight hesitation, a slow smile spread across his face. "True."

Cree moved past him, careful not to touch him because, deep down, that's exactly what she wanted to do. His nearness was wreaking havoc on her senses. She stepped back into the bedroom.

"What's this place going for, and how much is the HOA?"

"Eight million for the condo, and about ten grand a month for the HOA." He said it so nonchalantly Cree could only stare at him.

"Holy..."

Her gaze took in the space again. Yes, it was beautiful, but she wasn't sure if it was worth that. Granted, the views and the location probably accounted for much of that price, but still...

Cathy strolled into the room. "What do you two think, Tristan? Are you interested in putting in an offer?"

"Let me step out while you two talk," Cree said and made a hasty retreat.

She strolled back through the place, still in awe of its beauty, but looking at everything in a new light. The price tag reminded her of Tristan's net worth, or what she assumed it to be, and she smiled to herself. Again, she was so proud of what he had accomplished and was a bit in awe. He'd done it. He had reached a few of his goals that she knew about—financial wealth to support her and his family, the ability to live anywhere he wanted, and being able to buy any number of cars he desired.

It wasn't lost on her that this could've been her life. She

could be married to the world's greatest running back, or former running back, and wealthier than she'd ever dreamed possible. If they'd still been married, would she have still pursued her own goals? Like having a successful sports agency or law firm? Or like living in a beautiful home in Hinsdale or Lake Forest, Illinois?

Cree startled when she felt a hand on her hip. So caught up in her thoughts, she hadn't realized Tristan and his agent had returned to the living room.

"Ready?" he asked.

She glanced from him to the agent who had a small smile on her lips. "Sure, if you are. Did you make a decision?"

"Yeah, I'm going to pass on this place and keep looking."

"Really?" she asked, searching his eyes. He seemed to really like the place, but she guessed with having to make a quick decision, that probably didn't appeal to him.

He smirked. "Yes, really. Besides, though I could tell you liked it, you aren't in love with it."

She sighed. "Tristan," she started, but stopped since they had an audience.

She didn't want him making any decisions one way or another because of her. They weren't getting back together, and the sooner she made that clear the better.

But before she could say anything more, he said, "I know."

Cree wasn't sure what he thought he knew, but she hoped they were on the same page. They couldn't go back. Yes, what they once had together was amazing, a dream come true, and she could admit she missed Tristan like crazy.

However, she was a different person. Heck everything was different now, and there was no way they could pick up where they'd left off.

Could they?

Those two words popped into her head, bounced around a few minutes, and then she shook them free.

Nope, they couldn't. That was in the past. There was no more making plans to buy a house, have a couple of kids, and live happily ever after. They missed their chance, even though there was a tiny part of her that kept whispering, *What if?*

Chapter Ten

"I still think this is a bad idea," Cree said as she punched in the code that would get them into the underground parking lot of Tristan's apartment complex.

Since he only lived a few blocks from the condo that they'd just toured, he had walked there. That ended up being a good decision once he talked Cree into giving him a ride home. Not only that, he suggested they review the offers while she was there.

"Why is it a bad idea?" Tristan taunted from the passenger seat. He could get used to her chauffeuring him around, even if she did threaten to put him out a couple of times. "Are you afraid you won't be able to keep your hands off me? I can understand that. I am irresistible," he teased and cracked up when she rolled her eyes at him.

"Just stop dreaming and tell me where to park."

He directed her to the second row and to one of three of his parking spaces. She pulled in next to his Aston Martin, and it was a good thing too. The longer he sat beside her in this car, the more he wanted her.

It started back at the condo. Every touch and accidental brush of her body against his had been like an electrical charge shooting through his body. His desire for her was off the charts. It didn't matter that he had just seen her a couple of days ago. Each time in her presence made it harder to keep his hands and his mouth off her.

Tristan wanted to kiss her, and all he had to do was reach over the center console, pull her close, and capture her mouth in a searing kiss. Then if that went well, he could carry her off to his bedroom and make mad, passionate love to her all night long.

Yeah, that wouldn't be happening any time soon. But one day she'd be his again because there was no doubt in his mind that he was still in love with Cree Priestly. He never stopped loving her, and he just had to stay the course and win her back.

After Cree parked, she turned to him. "When we get inside, don't even think about trying any funny stuff," she said and narrowed her eyes at him. "Because I'm on to you. I know this is all a ploy to get me alone."

Tristan knew she was dead serious, yet he couldn't help but laugh. He laughed even harder when she punched him in the shoulder.

To most people, Cree was a total badass who moved around this world like she owned it. She also spoke her mind. Not that she was currently showing it, but so many people didn't get to see the other side of her. She was one of the most generous people he knew—with her money and her time—especially if she liked you. She might look like a beauty queen with her gorgeous hourglass figure, but she was also domestic. Cleaning, cooking, and she knew how to take care of her man.

God, he missed her.

"You laugh, but I'm serious, Tristan. There's no going back. So if you think you're wearing me down, think again. Like I said, I'm on to you. We have a business agreement, nothing else. Are we clear?"

"Yes! Now can we go inside?"

Tristan didn't bother waiting for her response. He hurried out of the car, then opened the driver's side door for her. Today she wasn't wearing a suit. No, instead, she had on a navy-blue wrap dress with a deep neckline, and the material hugged her sexy figure to perfection.

She used to hate working out, but clearly, she was doing something to stay in shape. The moment she stepped out of the car, the dress opened slightly to show a smooth, shapely thigh, and Tristan swallowed hard.

Yeah, he couldn't wait to be reacquainted with her. The woman was cover-girl beautiful, wicked smart, and self-confident in everything she did. She was truly the complete package. A package he looked forward to unwrapping again. Hopefully, before Christmas.

He wanted his wife back.

No other woman twisted him up inside or made him feel alive and desired in the way she looked at him when she was checking him out. After today, there was no doubt they were still attracted to one another, but he wanted more. He wanted her to fall in love with him again.

When he unlocked the door to his apartment, Cree strolled inside. He stood back as she glanced around, and he wondered what she thought of the place. When she moved over to the huge built-in bookcases, Tristan's chest puffed out as she took in his awards and trophies.

Playing football had been his lifelong dreams, and his career had given him everything he ever dreamed of and more. Except one thing. Cree. Without her to share the highs and even the lows with, his life hadn't been complete.

She slowly moved around the large space, taking in the

leather furniture, oversize television mounted on the wall, and views of the city. As apartments went, this one was nice and grand in the eyes of most people. Yet, he typically lived in places grander and more lavishly decorated. Though he wasn't planning on staying there long, he liked how comfortable it was despite downtown's congestion.

"A piano?" she asked and approached the baby grand that he had purchased years ago. It sat in the corner near the window, so when he was playing, he could stare out into the city.

"Yeah, I started taking piano lessons during the off season. I always wanted to learn to play, and now I find playing relaxes my mind."

She stared at him with an expression he couldn't decipher, but there was no doubt she was shocked by the revelation. Outside of his family and close friends, very few people knew he played.

"There's a lot you don't know about me, Cree."

"Clearly," she murmured, and he was sure there were things he didn't know about her, but he planned on changing that.

"Would you like a tour?" Tristan asked, noting she was still taking in the living room-kitchen combo. At twenty-five hundred square feet, the place was way smaller than he was accustomed to, but it worked for his current needs.

"No. I won't be here long. I just want to go over these offers with you," she said, patting the side of her large bag. "Where do you want to talk?"

"In the kitchen. I'm starving. Do you want anything to eat or drink?"

After rinsing his hands in the sink, Tristan pulled out the leftover lasagna he made the day before, along with garlic bread and the fixings for a salad.

"Water would be great," she said and sat at the island on one of the leather bar stools. She pulled the documents from her bag and sat them on the counter next to her.

Tristan grabbed a bottle of water from the refrigerator, twisted the top and handed it to her.

Once his food was ready, he set everything on the counter and glanced at Cree. She was eyeing his lasagna, and he tried not to smile. It was his specialty and a dish he knew she loved. Instead of asking her again if she wanted something to eat, he shoveled a fork full of lasagna into his mouth.

"Okay, which offer do you want to start with?" he asked, not missing how she kept stealing glances at his meal.

"I can't believe you're eating in front of me like that," she snapped. "Can't you wait until I leave?"

"No. I can't. I'm a big man. I need to fuel this body every couple of hours."

She slowly let her gaze travel the length of him, and the appreciation he saw in her eyes made him want to flex his muscles. It wasn't the first time he had caught her checking him out today. The way she was looking at him right now, he was tempted to take off his shirt and really give her something to look at. The twenty-one-year-old body she'd seen years ago had morphed into a well-oiled machine with five percent body fat.

"It looks good," she said, licking her lips, and he groaned. He wanted to be the one licking her lips.

Needing to get his mind off her mouth, he asked, "You talkin' about me or the food?"

"The food. Definitely the food."

Tristan smirked. Not sure if she'd accept his offer, he loaded the fork up with food and brought it to her mouth.

Cree's left brow lifted, and she stared at him, but then she shocked the hell out of him when she opened for him. She held his gaze as he fed her, and his dick twitched at the way she slowly chewed the food. As if savoring every single spice.

If she was trying to turn him on, it was working. Hell, it didn't take much since he'd been sporting a semi-erection since the moment he saw her outside of the condo. But when she moaned and closed her eyes while chewing, he almost lost it. Now she was just messing with him.

"*Cree*," he said in a low growl, and her eyes popped open.

"What?" She covered her mouth slightly with her hand as she continued chewing. "I can't help it if it's good, and it's sooo good. Can I have some more?"

Tristan shook his head and chuckled. "I thought you didn't want anything to eat," he said as he fed her more.

"That was before I knew you made lasagna."

As he continued feeding them both, Cree started going over the offers. He had time to think about the coaching offers, but he needed to make decisions regarding the endorsement deals. Cree gave suggestions and made notes as they talked.

Tristan knew his worth when it came to being a star running back with the NFL, but it was mind-boggling to see companies offering him millions to endorse their brands and products.

He had come a long way from growing up on the Southside of Chicago in one of the roughest neighborhoods. Back then, his parents, each working two jobs, had barely made enough to keep food on the table and a roof over his and his siblings' heads. Now he made more in a year than most people made in a lifetime.

"I'm not sure how thoroughly you went through this document," she said, lifting a page for him to see it was the one from a popular, sports apparel company. "But they want to film several campaigns at once, which would explain the amount of money they're offering. And they want to film in Atlanta."

Tristan sighed. He'd thought it would be one commercial and a photo shoot. Filming several commercials might take weeks, which would keep him from home and Cree. He'd done his share of commercials while playing football, and though some had been fun, they were also tedious with the retakes.

"How long are they saying it will take?" he asked.

"Minimum a week, but they don't think it'll take more than two weeks if all goes well. I'm not sure if that's true because they are planning to shoot in two different locations."

"What about the photo shoot?" he asked, biting into his garlic bread and trying not to moan. *Damn, this is delicious if I should say so myself.*

When he caught Cree looking at his mouth, or maybe she was looking at the bread, he held it out to her. He had offered her piece a few minutes ago, but she had declined. She claimed that, after all the lasagna, she didn't need more carbs.

"I don't know why you're trying to cut back on bread, but you're going to want to taste this. It'll be worth every calorie."

After a slight hesitation, she leaned in and took a large bite while he held it, and damn if that wasn't sexy. They were both big eaters and used to feed each other all the time. Just something else he missed about their time together.

Cree closed her eyes and moaned again, the sound making his body stir. He struggled to hold in his own moan as he watched her chew and then swallow. He wanted to pull her into his arms and kiss her so bad, but he couldn't. One wrong move this evening could mess up any progress he'd made with her so far. Yet, he wanted more than anything to feel her lush curves hugged up to him, and her sweet lips pressed against his.

"You're right. That was worth every calorie and so was the lasagna. I see you haven't lost your cooking skills."

"Baby, I'm a hundred percent better at everything," he said, holding her gaze and making sure she understood what he was saying. "Just let me know if you want to experience any of my other skills."

"*Tristan*," she said in a warning tone that also sounded like a whine.

She wanted him. Cree wanted him as bad as he wanted her, but she was still fighting the attraction.

"Are you dating anyone?" he asked.

"Not that it's any of your business, but no. I'm focusing on my career, and speaking of which, let's get back to this offer. Regarding filming in Atlanta, I talked to the director and the cinematographer earlier today about the schedule. One mentioned you'll have a couple of fittings before they start shooting. So, I'm thinking we should have them add something in the contract about you only being available for two weeks. Additional time can be negotiated if needed, especially since the photoshoot will need to be worked into the timeframe."

Tristan wiped his mouth with a napkin and sighed. "I'd prefer to only be there a few days, but since I don't want to have to go back and forth with filming, I guess I'm going to have to hope they stay on task." That would mean being away from her for weeks. He didn't want the progress he was making with her to regress. Unless...

"Actually, to ensure they stay on schedule, you could always go with me," Tristan said, and the more he thought about the idea, the more he loved it.

"Nope. Not going to happen," Cree said as she jotted a note in the margin.

"Why not? You love traveling."

She snorted and rolled her eyes at him. "How would you know? You and I were so broke, we didn't get a chance to do much traveling."

"True, but now I have the means to make sure you get to go anywhere in the world you want to go."

Tristan had planned to take her to New York on a shopping spree with the signing bonus he was promised when he had signed with Philadelphia. But that idea got crushed once she kicked his ass to the curb.

His plan had been to give her the world, except he never got the chance. Not only did he want to give it to her now, he owed her. She deserved so much more than just lunch, a trip, and a percentage of his contracts. If given the chance, he'd give her everything her heart desired.

"Besides, if you like shopping as much as you used to, you'll have time to do it while we're in Atlanta. Come with me. Your expenses will be covered, and I'll make sure you get in as much shopping as you want. And you'll get a chance to ride on a private jet."

The way her lips parted slightly before she quickly closed her mouth had him fighting a smile. Oh yeah. She was softening to the idea. Now to make sure she said yes.

He turned away from her and stood with his empty plate. "If you can't go to ensure they stay on task and get me out of there within a week, then I'll pass on that offer. I don't enjoy flying all over the place as much as I used to. Let's reject—"

"Fine, I'll consider it," she snapped, then stood and pointed at him. "If, and that's a big if, I do decide to go, you better believe I'm billing you for every second. You're paying for my time, my hotel room, my food, and if I do some shopping, don't be surprised when I send you that bill too."

Tristan grinned, knowing she was serious. The fact that she was even considering his request was a win. But he couldn't get too excited yet. Not until she said yes to everything he wanted from her, including marrying him again.

In the meantime, he had to tread lightly while he reminded her of how good they once were together, and not just in bed. Within a month of meeting her all those years ago, he had known she was the one for him. At the time, his future had been up in the air, but he had wanted her to be a part of it. Then everything got shot to hell with one wrong decision. Now here he was trying to rebuild a relationship with the only woman he's ever loved.

"Also, if I agree to this, if you try any funny stuff while we're traveling, I'm leaving your ass in Atlanta and coming home."

Tristan's lips quirked, and he walked toward her with his hand outstretched. "Deal." When Cree shook his hand, he pulled her into his arms, and she gasped.

"Let me go." She swatted his chest but wasn't trying very hard to get out of his hold. So he placed a kiss against her temple, then peppered a few along her jaw.

"Tristan, didn't I just tell you no funny stuff? That means no touching. No kissing. No nothing. Now I'm having second thoughts about going. I can already tell it's not a good—"

Tristan's mouth covered hers, smothering the rest of her words.

So much for treading lightly. This wasn't part of his plan for the evening, but being so close to Cree, talking and bantering like old times, he couldn't help himself. He had waited years to taste her again, and there was no way he was stopping until he got his fill.

Chapter Eleven

Hot damn! The man's kisses were as potent as she remembered, and Cree was defenseless to push him away. She wanted this. She wanted him more than she wanted anything else in this moment, and for a change, she had no intention of pulling away.

This wasn't her surrendering to Tristan. No, this was her acting like a woman who hadn't been kissed this thoroughly in like forever. It had been months since she'd been with a man, and she yearned for the attention. Not just any attention, but attention from the only man she had ever loved—Tristan.

Some rational part of her mind was telling her to stop and move away from temptation. Yet, all her girlie parts were cheering her on, encouraging her to keep going and take all she wanted.

Cree slowly ran her hands up Tristan's torso, marveling at the way his sinewy muscles contracted beneath her touch. Once her arms were around his neck, he backed her against a wall without breaking contact and deepened their connection.

As he loved on her mouth, his hardness pressed against her,

and memories of them together like this flooded Cree's mind. Tristan had always been a great kisser and a generous lover, and he was currently reminding her of what she'd been missing. Him. This. The bond they once shared. All of it.

She lifted her leg, wrapping it around his hip and forcing him closer. He held her leg in place and rubbed his body against her. Desire pulsed through her as so many sensations swirled inside of her at the way Tristan was kissing her, touching her, and turning her on.

His other hand slid under the split of her wrap dress, and the second his calloused fingers caressed her thigh, bolts of electricity charged through her body. Cree wanted him in every way a woman could want a man, and that intensified when his hand moved to one of her butt cheeks. She moaned against his lips as he squeezed, kneading her flesh while grinding against her.

"Damn, you know how much I love you in a thong. Your fine ass," he murmured.

The feel of his thick erection against her stomach made it clear they wanted the same thing—to get naked and reacquaint themselves with each other's body.

He eased his mouth from hers and brushed his lips over her jaw. The sweet kisses continued along her cheek, beneath her ear, and on down to her neck.

Cree whimpered, needing more. It had been way too long since she'd been touched like this, and her sex starved body couldn't take much more of his teasing.

Tristan released a primal growl as he worked his way back up her body until he was staring into her eyes. His breath was coming in short spurts when he said, "I want you. I want you so damn bad. If that's not what you—"

"Yes," she said breathlessly and cupped his face between

her hands before covering his mouth with hers. Yes, she wanted him, and she wanted him now.

He had just picked her up and turned with her in his arms when the door alarm chimed, interrupting the quietness in the apartment. They both froze. But when they heard the door close, Tristan set her down so quickly, Cree almost lost her balance.

They were both still breathing hard as he turned his back to her, standing in front of her as if shielding her from a threat. When he reached back, his large hand resting on her hip, Cree wasn't sure if he was trying to keep her in place or if he was touching her to ensure she was still with him. His body was tense, like he was planning to lunge at the first sign of trouble.

"Tristan, are you..." A woman's voice filled the space, and now Cree was the one tensing.

What the hell? Some woman had a key to his apartment? She was about to shove him away, but before she could, Tristan moved with the speed of light away from her.

"Dammit, Bethany! How the hell are you just walking into my place without knocking?" Tristan ground out, looking like he wanted to strangle her. "What the hell are you doing here, and how'd you even get in?"

"Hello to you too, Big Brother."

Big brother?

Cree forgot he had a younger sister. She had never met her, but she'd heard about her. When she and Tristan were dating, Cree had insisted on keeping their relationship private. Meaning, most of their family didn't know about them. Which Tristan hated, but she'd been determined to build her sports agency without anyone questioning her integrity. She hadn't been willing to risk anyone finding out she'd been dating her client. And after they got married... Well, their marriage didn't last long enough for them to tell anyone what they'd done.

"I asked you a question," Tristan growled, and Cree couldn't ever remember seeing him this angry before. "How the hell did you get into my apartment?"

Bethany didn't seem phased by his anger. Instead, her focus was on Cree, and the woman narrowed her eyes. "Who are you?" she asked.

"None of your damn business!" Tristan barked.

Making sure her dress was closed, Cree moved away from the wall. "I'm going to run to the bathroom and give you two a minute."

She wasn't sure where the bathroom was, but she headed down a hallway until she came to one. She stepped into it and closed the door before leaning against it.

Her heart was still beating a little fast, but her body temperature was slowly going back to normal after that intense make-out session.

She breathed in deeply and released the breath slowly. Had she and Tristan not been interrupted, there was no doubt they would've done much more than just kiss. Maybe she should be thanking Bethany for interrupting. Then again, part of her wanted to go back out there and kick the twerp's ass for stopping what would've led to an epic time between the sheets.

"It was probably for the best," she mumbled and pushed away from the door.

When Cree reached the vanity, she glanced in the mirror at herself. Her hair was disheveled, her face was flushed, her dress was twisted, and most of her lipstick was gone. She looked like a woman who had been thoroughly kissed.

What the hell was she thinking kissing Tristan? Actually, she hadn't been thinking. She'd only been feeling. He was not the type of man you could just kiss once and walk away from. He was an addiction, one that stood the chance of being impossible to break.

Cree shook her head. "I gotta get out of here."

She wetted one of the paper hand towels and dabbed at her face and neck. Once she finished cooling down and righting her clothes, Cree left the bathroom.

"I gave you the key temporarily so you could let the cable person in. Not for you to walk into my place whenever the hell you want. Give me the key. Now!" he growled.

"Tristan, why are you tripping? It's not like I haven't seen you with one of your little groupies before."

"Give me the damn key, and call her a groupie again, and I'll disown your bratty ass."

As Cree moved closer, Bethany's gaze landed on her, and she didn't look too happy. It took a lot to piss Tristan off. Cree figured there must be more at play here, but she had no intention of sticking around to find out.

"Sorry to interrupt," she said, "but I'm gonna just grab my bag and head out."

She eased around Tristan and went into the kitchen for her handbag that she had set on one of the barstools. When she strolled back to where they were standing, Tristan stopped her with a touch on her hip. Facing her, he blocked her view of his sister.

"Cree, you don't have to leave. My sister—"

"*Cree?*" Bethany said, moving so Cree could see her. "So, you're the one."

Cree frowned. "The one what?"

"Bethany," Tristan said in a warning tone.

Now Cree really wanted to know what she was about to say.

"*Cree...*" Bethany said, nodding to herself, and Cree could tell she was working something out in her mind. "You're the mystery woman. The one who broke my brother's heart, aren't you? Years ago, he came home totally wasted one night and was mumbling something about not being able to live without *Cree*. It was you. You're the one who had him talking about giving up football."

Cree's heart sank. Shocked by Bethany's words, she looked at Tristan, and he was glaring at his sister.

"That's enough, Bethany," he said through gritted teeth.

"I always wondered who you were since he hadn't brought you around the family. So what, you're back to break his heart again?" Bethany asked before turning her attention to her brother. "Is she the reason you're kicking the family out of the house now? If she is the one who was stupid enough to leave you before, why would you think she wouldn't—"

"Enough!" Tristan stomped past Cree and gently grabbed his sister by the arm, tugging her toward the door. "It's time for you to go."

Cree didn't miss the wicked smirk on the woman's face, which only pissed Tristan off more.

"Wait," Cree said and pulled on the back of his shirt. "Don't. I was just leaving. I'll, um, I'll talk to you tomorrow."

"Cree, baby, you don't have to leave," Tristan pleaded and grasped her hand.

She swallowed hard, feeling like crap about what had happened years ago. If what his sister said was true, it would've killed Cree if Tristan had given up football. She might've been angry with him at the time, but she would have never wanted him to forgo his dream because of her.

She squeezed his hand and gave him a small smile. She wanted to stay, but it would be a bad idea. It was good they were interrupted. Their professional relationship was already on shaky ground. If they had added sex to the mix, she wasn't sure what would've happened afterwards.

Cree pulled her hand from his grasp. "We'll talk soon. Have a good night."

As she hurried down the hallway, she heard Bethany ask, *"Who exactly is she?"*

Cree doubted Tristan would tell her anything, but what if he did? What if he told her she was his ex-wife? He had always hated keeping their relationship a secret. Would he tell everyone about their past?

Chapter Twelve

So many thoughts swirled inside Cree's mind. The kiss. How right it felt to be with Tristan again. The secrets that she'd kept over the years. One scenario after another flooded her brain as she drove to her sister's house. She needed to talk this out, and since Essence knew her and Tristan's history, she'd understand why this was all so complicated.

But that kiss, though. That hadn't been just a kiss. Nope, it was a reminder of what she and Tristan once shared. Him and that lip-lock was everything Cree told herself she no longer wanted but everything she had missed.

He had always been easy to be around, and she was amazed at how simple it had been to fall right back into how things used to be between them. Hanging out talking, laughing, and eating together, feeding one another, and the banter. It all felt so natural.

But now, the desire, passion, and longing swirling inside of her was something she hadn't experienced in a long time. Not since...

Not since Tristan.

Cree shook her head. "Man..." She hadn't felt this way since they'd been together all those years ago. There wasn't a man on the planet who could turn her on like Tristan. She used to think he'd been made specifically for her, and after spending the last couple of hours with him, she still believed it.

Which was a problem. A big problem.

Cree squeezed the steering wheel tighter as she drove through the streets of Chicago. Getting involved with Tristan again was a horrible idea. However, she wanted him more than she had ever wanted anything in her life. But she didn't want to still be attracted to him. However, all the old feelings for him were back, and it was impossible to ignore them.

"What the heck am I going to do?"

A short while later, Cree stood on her sister's doorstep and rang the doorbell.

Essence opened the door almost immediately. "*Finally.* Where have you—"

"He kissed me, and I liked it," Cree whined, interrupting whatever her sister was about to say as she stomped past her and into the house. But Cree pulled up short when she reached the living room. "Ahh hell."

"Soooo, he kissed you, huh?"

"And you *liked* it!"

Her sisters, Dorian and Nyla said at the same time, then burst out laughing.

Raven, their sister-in-law ran into the room from the kitchen. "Wait! What did I miss?" In her hands were a charcuterie board and a plate of what looked to be three types of homemade cookies. "Who's been kissing who?"

"Yeah, that's what we want to know," Nyla, Cree's most outspoken and pain in the butt sister, said. "And just think, I thought we'd only be talking wedding stuff tonight."

"Wait. Oh, my goodness! Is this about your mystery man?

The one we ran into at the boutique weeks ago?" Dorian asked, looking hopeful.

"Ugh! I just can't with you guys tonight." Cree did an about face and started for the front door. So focused on talking to Essence, she hadn't scanned the street out front. Otherwise, she probably would've seen their cars.

Before Cree could leave, Essence blocked her path.

"You're here now. You might as well come in and join the rest of us for *girls' night*. You know, the night that has been planned for two weeks, and the one that you're an hour late for."

"Crap. I forgot."

"Clearly," Dorian said from behind her, and Cree turned to glare at her youngest sister. At some point, she had moved across the room and now stood a couple of feet behind her. "You can't leave now Cree. We want to know who you've been swapping spit with."

"Oh, my gawd. You've been spending too much time with Nyla because that sounds like some crap she would say!" Cree grumbled and rubbed her forehead, trying to decide if she should stick around or get out now.

She moved away from the front door and stood on the edge of the living room. The last thing she wanted to do was share her personal business. But she might not have a choice considering the way four sets of eyes were watching her.

Nyla poured tequila into two shot glasses, then crossed the room wearing an oversized suit jacket, a sports bra beneath it, and ripped jeans along with combat boots. "How about a little liquid courage to get you started?"

Cree huffed out a breath and took one of the glasses. She clinked it against Nyla's, then slammed it back, cringing as the strong liquor burned its way down the back of her throat. And already, it was helping.

She handed the glass back to her sister. "Make it a double, and I'll stick around."

"Deal."

Cree followed Nyla farther into the living room, dropped down in the recliner, and threw back a second shot.

"Now, start talking," Raven said as she piled snack food onto a small plate. The others did the same, and Cree marveled at how well their sister-in-law fit with the family. It was like she'd been a Priestly forever.

She and Cree's brother, Zion, had first met in Vegas. Their one-night stand produced a set of the most adorable twins, but Zion and the rest of the family hadn't found out until recently. While in Vegas, he and Raven had only exchanged first names. So when she later learned she was pregnant, she had no way of reaching him. Thankfully, fate played a hand at them running into each other at Cree's family's bed and breakfast. Needless to say, they were all shocked by the news, but Raven and the kids were a gift.

Cree fixed a plate, loaded it with cheese, crackers, pepperoni, and a few grapes. No one spoke as she took her time piling on the food while deciding how much to share. The tequila did its job. She felt more relaxed than she had all day, and her mind was clearer. Clear enough to come up with a way to buy herself some time.

"I'll share a little about my mystery man, but only after Dorian tells us what's going on with the wedding."

"Seriously, Cree? You do realize you were over an hour late getting here," Nyla snapped. "We already talked all things weddings. You're just stalling."

"So Dorian, how are the plans going?" Cree asked, ignoring Nyla who threw a handful of grapes at her.

"I hope you know you're cleaning that up," Essence said in what they referred to as her momma voice while she glared at

Nyla. "What you're not going to do is come in here throwing food. Now pick it up!"

Nyla dropped to her knees to pick up the grapes, and Cree couldn't stop the smile that spread across her face.

"Cree, quit playing around and tell them," Essence said, and Cree huffed out a breath.

"Fine. You guys know I don't like people in my business. So if I tell you what's going on, you have to promise to keep it to yourself. You can't even tell your husbands or soon to be husbands. Do we have a deal?"

"Come on, Cree! You know if I told Harrison to keep it to himself, he wouldn't say anything."

"The same with Lynix," Dorian said, frowning. "What is it? Did you kill someone?"

"Cree, I have a feeling, Tristan is here to stay," Essence said quietly. "Just tell them."

Cree kept her mouth shut. All these years she'd been able to keep her secrets from her family, but Essence was right. Tristan wasn't going anywhere, and Cree knew her resolve was weakening where he was concerned. She just didn't know what she'd do with him yet.

Raven threw up her hands. "Fine. We won't say anything, and I won't tell your brother. Just spill it."

"She's right, we'll keep your secrets. Now who's the mystery man?" Dorian asked. "I've been dying to know since seeing him at Jada's boutique."

"Fine. His name is Tristan Whitmore... and he's my ex-husband."

Chapter Thirteen

Cree almost laughed at her sisters' wide eyes and mouths hanging open. She knew she could trust them, but she just wasn't good at sharing. Maybe it was time she stopped making a big deal about the past and tell them a little about her and Tristan.

"What?"

"Seriously?"

"No way!"

Everyone spoke at once, and before Cree could respond, more questions were thrown her way.

"When did this happen?"

"How old were you?"

"Oh my God! How did we not know you were married?"

"And you're divorced? What's up with that?"

"Wait!" Raven yelled, waving her hands to get everyone's attention and silence fell over the room. "All I want to know is —does your mom know?"

Cree couldn't help but laugh. Their mom was a force to be

reckoned with, and she made it her business to know every-thing about her kids. But Cree's marriage was one of several things that most people didn't know.

"Ha! If Mom knew, we all would've known. So, how'd you keep the secret all this time?" Nyla asked.

"Oh, boy. Mom's going to be disappointed when she finds out," Dorian said and then grinned. "She's back to her match-making schemes and planned to introduce you to the youth pastor at her church."

Cree rolled her eyes and sighed. She thought her mother was done with her matchmaking schemes. She'd been making her way through the five of them, and Cree wasn't having it. Poor Dorian recently had to put up with that nonsense, but it worked out. Their mom unknowingly pushed her right into Lynix's arms. Granted, Lynix hadn't been the man their mother wanted for her baby girl, but he was perfect for her.

"How did you and Tristan meet?" Dorian asked.

Cree told her sisters how she and Tristan had run into each other at a club. Used to being hit on, she rarely gave out her number, but there was something about Tristan that intrigued her. Even more so after the first time they talked on the phone well into the next morning. That was a first for Cree, and the more she got to know him, the harder she fell for him.

But Tristan had been a few years younger than her, and they'd been at different stages in their lives. She honestly hadn't thought the relationship would last, which was why she hadn't introduced him to her family. Yet, they clicked.

"You ever meet someone who makes your whole body come alive whenever you're in their presence? You miss them when they aren't near you, and you count down the days, the minutes, and even the seconds until you see them again."

"Yes," her sisters said in unison.

"Well, that's Tristan for me."

"Don't think I didn't catch you saying that in present tense," Raven said grinning. "So even after all these years, the feelings are still the same?"

Cree sighed as she pondered the question. The easy answer was yes, but she wasn't sure if it was really him twisting her up inside and making her want what they used to have. Or if it had more to do with the fact that it had been a long time since she'd been with a man.

Then again, her heart still beat a little faster whenever Tristan was around, and the tingling sensation that swirled inside of her just thinking about him spoke volumes.

"Why does his name sound so familiar?" Raven asked, a frown on her face as she typed into her cell phone, no doubt Googling him.

"He plays football, and your husband is a fan of his," Essence said.

Raven snapped her fingers. "That's right! Zion mentioned winning money in the past with his fantasy football, and it was thanks to Tristan. Oh, and this brotha is *fiiiine!*" she said, showing Nyla and Dorian the picture of Tristan that she'd found online.

"Dang, Sis. I'm shocked you were able to walk away from all that," Nyla cracked.

"And he looks even better in person," Dorian added.

Raven squealed. "Zion is going to freak when he finds out you not only know Tristan Whitmore, but you were married to him!"

"But he's not going to find out just yet, right?" Cree said firmly, eyeing each one of them.

If she and Tristan reunited, she wouldn't be able to keep their relationship a secret this time around.

"Oh, yeah, that's right. My lips are sealed," her sister-in-law said and pretended to zip her lips.

"I had a feeling when I saw him that day at the boutique that he played some type of sport. The man is huge," Dorian said. "But why'd you guys break up? When we ran into him at the boutique, you looked as if you wanted to smack him."

Cree snorted. "At the time, I did. I was shocked to see him because it had been years."

"So what happened?" Nyla asked, stuffing her face with food.

"Shortly after I started my sports agency, Tristan became one of my clients. Which complicated our relationship."

Cree explained she had recently graduated from law school when she started her sports agency. Tristan was attending the University of Chicago and playing football for the school. He'd wanted more than anything to get into the NFL, and she honestly thought it was a long shot. Still Cree took him on as a client.

"I tried breaking up with him then, but he wasn't having it." Cree smiled, thinking about how convincing Tristan could be when he wanted something.

"Dang, I can't wait to meet this guy if he has you over there smiling like that. Your scowls usually hide your smiles," Nyla said laughing, and Cree rolled her eyes while biting down on her lower lip to squash her smile.

When it came to Tristan, it had always been hard to hide her feelings whether she was happy with him or mad at him. There was just something about the guy who could turn her on one minute and then make her want to punch him the next.

"When I signed him to my agency, I didn't want anyone to know we were dating, especially while I was trying to get my business going. We'd only been together a few months at the time, and I was all about being a professional while I drummed up more clients."

Then she landed him a contract with Chicago, making both of their dreams come true. It was peanuts compared to what NFL players receive today, but they'd both been thrilled. After that, Tristan had put in the work, proving he'd be a star one day. Cree knew she could get him a bigger contract the following season, but he signed with the other agent.

"Dang. No wonder you were pissed at him," Nyla said. "Considering you used to fight first and ask questions later, I'm surprised the guy is still alive."

"*Right?*" Dorian co-signed and laughed with the others. "I can't believe he'd just up and sign with someone else, knowing he'd be hurting you."

"In his defense, I can't much blame him. The other agent had a ton of experience in the industry and could get him more money. Tristan recently told me that he knew I'd be mad at the news, but he thought I'd understand it was business. With him getting a larger contract, we both would win, especially since we were married."

"But you didn't see it that way," Essence said, a sympathetic expression marring her face. "I wish you guys could've talked it all out before ending the marriage."

Cree shrugged. "Yeah, woulda, shoulda, coulda. I was young, dumb, and in my feelings. I wasn't trying to hear anything he had to say."

"So when are we going to meet this guy?" Dorian asked. "Will he be at your birthday party next month?"

Cree had planned to celebrate her thirty-seventh birthday at Moody Days Jazz Club that her sister Nyla owned. She had only invited her siblings, a few friends, and the employees at the spa. She hadn't considered inviting Tristan. Part of her wanted to, but if she did, it would go against her policy of not mixing business with pleasure.

"I don't know," she said honestly. "I'm not sure I want to risk it."

"Risk what?" Raven asked.

Cree told them what she had explained to Tristan—that she'd represent him, but there couldn't be anything between them personally. She'd done that once, and she hated how things turned out. Besides, she had too much to lose. Integrity was everything to her, and if it came out that she was dating a client, a high-profile one at that, it wouldn't be a good look for her professionally.

"Does the firm have a rule about their lawyers or partners dating clients?" Essence asked.

"It's highly discouraged."

"Even though you guys used to be married?" Essence asked.

Cree shrugged. Their previous relationship would make a difference, but still...

"I've worked my ass off to build my clientele list as well as become partner. I don't want anything to overshadow what I've accomplished. Besides, attorneys shouldn't date their clients. It's just not a good look and can compromise the business relationship and could be a conflict of interest."

"Well, it's a stupid rule... or a stupid unspoken rule," Dorian said with a flippant wave of her hand.

Essence leaned forward and leveled Cree with a look. "You have a second chance with the only man you've ever loved. You and Tristan are made for each other, and it might be worth giving your relationship another chance. I've seen you two together."

"That was a long time ago, Sis," Cree said, her pulse amping at the thought of giving Tristan another chance. She wanted to. God, she wanted to, but the logical side of her brain was saying it was a bad idea and too big of a risk.

"It might've been a long time ago," Essence continued, "but I've never seen you happier than when you were with him. Isn't what you two once shared worth giving another try?"

"Isn't what you and Jackson share worth taking your relationship to the next level?" Cree shot back defensively, and someone in the room gasped. Surprisingly, the others didn't jump in since they all felt the same about Essence and Jackson.

"We're not talking about me. We're talking about you!" Essence said with some bite behind her words, which was a rarity. She was typically the cool, calm one in the group, mothering everyone. "And while we're on the subject, Cree, aren't you tired of keeping secrets? Does he even know about—"

"Essence!" Cree snapped, forcing her sister to stop talking before she said too much.

Anger swirled inside of Cree at what her sister was probably getting ready to say. There were some secrets Cree planned to take to her grave. And for Essence to almost reveal one meant she was really pissed. She got like that whenever Cree called her out about Jackson. Essence and Jackson were the best of friends, and he wanted to be more than friends. They got along like a happily married couple, and Jackson had always been like a father to Tray, who adored him. Yet, Essence wouldn't budge. She wasn't willing to be more than just friends with the man.

"Clearly we're missing a big piece of the puzzle," Nyla said, dividing her attention between Cree and Essence. "And I'd guess it's a very big piece."

"Does Tristan know you used to be a stripper?" Raven asked, and Cree growled under her breath.

"Yes, he knows," she ground out.

That had been a source of contention in their relationship,

mainly when someone recognized her. That didn't happen often since she used to wear a disguise when she worked at a strip club. The reddish wig and heavy makeup transformed her into someone totally different. Someone named Siren, which was Cree's stage name. Her alter ego was bold, edgy, and playful while also being mysterious. Cree hated stripping, but she enjoyed playing the role.

She had always been careful not to share her real name with anyone at the club. She had only stripped for a year, and never to the point of being completely nude. She'd only done it to help pay her way through law school, and it had been a profitable side hustle.

Her sisters and brother knew, as well as Tristan, about that time in her life, but it wasn't something Cree planned to share with anyone else.

"What's the other big secret you're keeping from us? Because I know there's something else, and it's something that Essence knows."

"I'm done talking," Cree snapped and stood. She wasn't leaving yet, but she needed air.

"Wait. I have one more question," Dorian said quickly, and Cree turned back to her. "Are you going to give Tristan a second chance? I don't know him, but if he was able to convince you, of all people, to marry him, he must be special."

That, Cree could agree with. Tristan was special and like no other man she'd ever met.

"I think you should give him another chance," Dorian added.

"I do too," Nyla and Raven said in unison.

Of course they did. They were all madly in love with their men and wanted everyone they knew to be just as in love.

For the first time in a long time, Cree imagined what it would be like to be happily married to her soulmate. She often said she didn't need a man, but if she was honest with herself, she wanted one. But only if it was Tristan.

"I don't know," Cree finally said, rubbing her forehead as a sudden bout of exhaustion settled over her. There was so much to consider, and right now, she didn't know what she'd do. So she said, "We'll see."

Chapter Fourteen

Tristan followed behind Quincy and Jamal's uncle like a lost puppy, and he couldn't seem to snap out of the disinterest that plagued him. They were touring the commercial building that his brother wanted them to purchase, and Jamal's uncle, the owner, dominated the conversation. He told them more than Tristan cared to know about the building and the tenants.

From what he had seen of the place so far, it was nice, but his heart wasn't into being social today. Mainly because almost every thought he'd had over the last few days were centered around Cree. He had no idea where he stood with her because she was back to business as usual.

Guilt plagued him. He just couldn't seem to get anything right with her, and it started years ago. Back then, he had lost her because he failed to communicate his intention of getting a new agent, even if the decision had been a good one. At least this time, the riff between them wasn't his fault, not totally. No, that honor went to his sister and her horrible timing and big mouth. All the progress he'd made with Cree had taken a nose-dive, and Tristan didn't know how to fix it.

Cree, who didn't embarrass easily, had told him that being caught like two teenagers making out in the back seat of a Chevy was extremely embarrassing. Especially at their age. It hadn't helped that Bethany had revealed that Cree had been the woman behind Tristan almost giving up on football.

Thanks to his sister, any progress of getting Cree back was probably destroyed, and he'd have to start his pursuit all over again. At least that's how it felt. Cree had accepted his apology but gave no clue as to where that left them. She made sure the few conversations they'd had since that day at his apartment centered around business, and he was sick of it.

"Since I knew I'd be selling the building, I didn't renew most of the leases," the owner said, cutting into Tristan's thoughts. "The info your accountant requested will show the building has been income-generating for the last twenty years. In this neighborhood, you won't have a problem leasing out the space. We housed a retail business on the main floor and an array of other businesses on the second and third floors."

They were currently near a set of elevators on the second floor, and Tristan finally started listening when the owner told them the type of companies that had leased the top floors. In his opinion, the building was way more space than they needed, but the idea of further diversifying his portfolio appealed to him. Owning a commercial building in a prime location near downtown Chicago might not be a bad idea. He never wanted to be a landlord, but if someone else was managing the place, buying commercial real estate could be a win.

"We can head up to the top floor that is currently being leased by a law firm. They are closed on Sundays, and it won't be a problem with us touring the space." As they rode the elevator, the landlord explained that the firm was one of the companies whose lease wasn't renewed. They'd be vacating at the end of this month.

A short while later, the owner unlocked the door to the law office and began showing them around. It was clear the firm had already started moving based on some of the empty spaces and packed boxes.

There was more space than Tristan expected, and he wondered if Quincy would use that floor for the nonprofit. Or if he would lease it to another law firm. Which would make more sense to Tristan. The nonprofit didn't need that large of a space.

As they went from one office to another, Cree popped into his mind again, but not because of the distance she'd put between them. No, he had an idea, and it was becoming clearer as he toured the office space.

There'd been a time when Cree's number one goal had been to own her own sports agency. But thanks to him, she'd had to close it. He wondered if she'd be interested in starting it back up, especially if he offered her office space and helped her build her clientele.

If not an agency, maybe she'd want to start her own law practice. Instead of a partner, she'd be an owner, and whatever tension he had witnessed between her and Warren would go away.

Tristan's pulse amped, and he was starting to feel more encouraged as the idea bloomed inside of him. Yeah, this could be his way of making things right between them, as it related to him bailing on her years ago. In the process, they could get their relationship back on track.

But first, he needed to find out her plans for the future, and he had to make sure they included him.

"So what do you think?" the owner asked, snapping Tristan back into the conversation.

Though they had driven separately, they had talked on the phone on the way to the property. Quincy had offered to take the lead, which was fine with Tristan. Ultimately, they'd both make the decision, but technically, it was his brother's idea to purchase a commercial building, then lease a portion of it to the nonprofit. Tristan had to admit—it was a good business decision.

"I like what I've seen, but we're not prepared to make a decision at this moment," Quincy said. "Once we review the numbers, I'll get back to you."

They took the steps to the ground floor, and while Quincy asked the owner a few more questions, Tristan stepped outside. A cool breeze whipped around him, and he zipped his leather jacket and pulled the wool cap he was wearing lower over his eyes.

The fall weather had gotten chillier over the last few days, but it was Chicago. This time of year, he was just glad it wasn't snowing.

He glanced around, noting the large amount of foot traffic, neighboring businesses, and the building's location on a busy street. All that might be a good sign as it related to attracting small businesses interested in leasing office space.

There was minimum parking out front, but the building came with a parking lot. Though small, it would still appeal to potential business owners.

Tristan had just turned to his left when two women exited the spa next door. They were laughing at something, and he froze when his attention landed on the tall one. Taking in the woman's short, camel colored coat and matching knee-high boots, he blinked several times wondering if his eyes were playing tricks on him.

Had his mind conjured up Cree?

When she turned slightly, giving him a better view of her profile, excitement leaped inside of him. *Fate.* It had to be fate, some supernatural power, that had them standing only a few feet apart.

"Okay, I'll talk to you next week," Cree said to the woman as they hugged goodbye. When her friend strolled away, Cree glanced down at her cell phone in her hand.

"Cree?" Tristan called out as he took a few steps toward her.

Her head jerked up, and she glanced in his direction, surprise registering on her face.

"Tristan, what are you doing here?"

He pointed toward the building that was for sale. "Touring the building. What about you?"

She gave a head nod to the spa. "Getting my hair and nails done."

He hadn't realized spas and salons were opened on Sundays, but why not? Busy professionals like her probably took advantage of the services on the weekend versus trying to squeeze in pampering during the weekdays.

As he looked at Cree, all he could think was that she was so beautiful, and it seemed she got more gorgeous with each passing day. Everything about her appearance was on point, from her sexy haircut with her long bangs swept over one eye, to her perfectly made-up face, on down to her chic outfit. She looked like she was ready to step out on the town, and he wanted to be right beside her when she did.

"Can we go somewhere and talk?" he asked, prepared for her to say no but hoping for a yes.

After a slight hesitation, she said, "I'm not sure that's a good idea. Besides, I already called for a ride."

"Cancel it. I'll cover whatever the cancellation fee is, and I'll make sure you get home safely."

She eyed him warily, then broke eye contact and glanced around at their surroundings. He wasn't sure what she was thinking, but her hesitation was a good thing. That meant she was considering his request.

Her attention returned to her cell phone, and he hoped she was canceling the ride.

"Please, Cree," Tristan said. He wasn't too proud to beg and would do anything to spend some time with her. "Let's go somewhere and talk."

She looked at him and shocked the hell out of him when she nodded. "Okay, but I pick the place this time."

Tristan grinned. "Deal."

Chapter Fifteen

Tristan helped Cree out of his Aston Martin and after closing the door, he settled his hand at the small of her back. *Goodness.* An involuntary shiver scurried up her spine as they strolled across the parking lot to the Thai restaurant.

Cree shouldn't be enjoying his touch so much, but it was hard not to. That, as well as the enticing scent of his woodsy cologne she'd had to endure during the fifteen-minute drive, had her wanting to skip lunch and go straight to bed.

So yeah, she should really move out of his hold, put some space between them because the heat spreading through her body had her self-control teetering. This was not how she was supposed to be thinking or feeling about her *client*, but Essene might've been right. Getting involved with Tristan might be a big risk, but he was worth it. Besides, she missed him.

When they entered the restaurant, the sweet, tangy, savory, aroma of spices greeted them at the door, and Cree's stomach growled. Her protein bar for breakfast had worn off, and she was starving. They might be there to talk, but she couldn't wait to eat.

She glanced around. The exposed brick walls, hardwood floors, and minimum lighting added to the coziness of the place. The establishment wasn't very busy, but Cree requested a table near the back of the dining room. She wasn't sure if anyone would recognize Tristan, especially with his cap pulled low on his head. Still, a true fan might know it's him, and the last thing she wanted was for them to end up on someone's social media page.

"Are you embarrassed to be seen with me?" Tristan asked quietly once they were seated.

On the contrary, she wanted to say. She was glad to be with him. Being with him evoked memories of love, desire, and passionate nights. Her memory bank was busting at the seams, and now she wanted what they once had when they couldn't keep their hands off each other.

Instead of saying any of that, though, she said, "No, but I have a few concerns. You're a household name now, and in the days of people using the camera on their cell phones to snap photos, I don't want to end up in one with you. No offense," she hurried and added. "I'm just an attorney having lunch with my client."

His lips twitched, and his sexy brown eyes sparkled. "Well, just so you know, I'm counting this as our first date. As for you not wanting to be in a photo with me, what are you going to do when we officially start dating?"

She narrowed her eyes at him even though her heart leaped in anticipation. "I never said anything about dating you officially."

"You didn't have to. It's only a matter of time, baby. You won't be able to resist much longer," he said and grinned.

"Cocky much?" she ground out.

No way would she tell him he was right because she was still trying to come to terms with her decision about him. Hooking up with him would be life-altering in more ways than one. She had to be sure. She'd always been a bit reckless when it came to Tristan and apparently, considering how much she wanted him, age and wisdom hadn't changed that.

The server took their drink order, and since they knew what they wanted to eat, they ordered their entrees as well. A short while later, the woman returned with Cree's glass of red wine and Tristan's beer.

As Cree sipped her merlot, she watched Tristan over the rim of the glass. He was looking around the restaurant, oblivious of her taking him in. He really was a handsome man with smooth honey-brown skin. She normally liked him clean-shaven, but the five o'clock shadow he was sporting on his cheeks and chin was a good look on him. It added to his ruggedness and sex appeal.

"I'm surprised you're not somewhere watching football," she said.

"I would've been if Quincy hadn't been insistent on me touring that building."

As Tristan told her about his nonprofit, pride swelled inside of Cree. She was so proud of the man he had become and loved how he was giving back to those less fortunate. Most professional athletes did that to some degree, but Tristan's nonprofit supported not only the kids in sports, but also the parents.

An arm of the nonprofit helped with living expenses and emergencies. So, they weren't just taking care of the athlete but also the family. They understood that, if the child's home life wasn't stable, it would affect their abilities in whatever sport they were playing.

"I love what you guys are doing," she said.

"Good. That means you'll attend the next fundraiser and

give a huge donation," Tristan cracked, and Cree laughed.

"I didn't say all that," she joked, but looked forward to attending and donating.

"Okay, we have the Pad Thai and a side order of Tom Yum Goong for you," the server said with a heavy accent and set the dishes in front of Cree. "And for you," she said to Tristan, "we have the Khao Pad with chicken. Anything else?"

Cree shook her head no, but Tristan requested water for them both.

Silence fell between them for the first few bites of their meal, but then he asked about the spa. He'd been surprised it was open on Sundays. As a silent partner, Cree stayed out of the day-to-day operations and was pleased at how the business was being run. But at the last business meeting, she had suggested offering a few services on Sundays. Her business partner thought it was a great idea and implemented it soon after. According to their bottom line, the suggestion was paying off.

"A badass boss lady," Tristan said with a smile. "You never cease to amaze me. I recall you talked about one day opening a spa with your college roommate. So, you guys finally did it. Congratulations."

Cree couldn't help but grin. She was proud of them, but hearing Tristan's praise meant a lot.

"Coming here was a good choice," he said. "The food is excellent."

Cree agreed and tried not to eat so fast, but her dish was delicious. It had the perfect balance of noodles, peanuts, and fresh vegetables. Add that with the sweet, salty and savory spices, and she had the perfect meal.

"What do you do in your free time?" Tristan asked.

"Lately, I haven't had much free time, but when I do get some, I hang out with family, specifically my sisters. Oh, and now I have a niece and nephew, twins, who I spend time with when I can."

"Nice! Whose kids?"

"My brother, Zion, and his wife, Raven."

Cree told him about how the two got together and what a shock it had been for Zion and the family to learn about the twins. Though Tristan hadn't met her family, he knew about them. She filled him in on the new marriages, as well as Dorian and Lynix's recent engagement.

When she was done talking about her family, he gave her updates on his. His siblings hadn't married yet, nor did he have any nieces or nephews. He explained how he was selling some of his properties around the country while looking for a new place for his parents, as well as himself.

"Sounds like you've been busy. Now that you're retired, have you done anything fun?" Cree asked.

He shook his head. "Not really. More than anything, I've been trying to get settled in. I always knew I'd return to Chicago, but I didn't realize how hard it would be to leave Philly. It was my second home, and I made some good friends and connections while there. I'm even missing the fans a little."

"I bet. With them bowing down to you wherever you go, I can see how it would be hard to leave that type of attention."

Tristan chuckled. "The notoriety has its pros and cons. Most of the fans have been cool. Every now and then, a jerk will try to start some mess but overall, they're okay. I'll miss some aspects of the fame, but I won't miss some of the reporters who twist the truth and make up their own narratives."

Cree listened as he told her about the uproar that surrounded him and a few other players a few years ago. They'd been accused of betting on several NFL games, and though some of them had, Tristan insisted he had never bet on any professional sport.

"It was a mess. I ended up filing a defamation suit against the reporter and the media outlet who spewed that nonsense. We settled out of court, and they had to make a public apology. I've tried to stay clear of reporters since then or risk knocking someone the hell out.

"But anyway, now that I've been forced into retirement, I'm trying to decide what I'll do with the next chapter of my life."

Cree understood why he hadn't wanted to retire yet. He was still in his prime but retiring at such a young age with enough money to live on, he could do whatever he wanted. Including starting a new career.

While they continued eating, small talk flowed easily between them. Tristan told her about how hard it had been to come to terms with his injuries after his last professional football game. Cree could hear the despair in his tone, and it sounded like his injuries and his recovery had been a lot worse than the media had reported.

"I'm glad you're okay now, but that all had to be scary. I hate you had to experience that," she said, meaning every word.

"Yeah, it was the second worst time in my life," he said as he ate and stared down at his plate as he spoke. "The first time was losing you."

He didn't look at her when he spoke those words, and Cree's heart squeezed. Normally, she'd change the subject, but it was time they discussed what happened back then. Not necessarily why they broke up, but what happened after the fact. Or at least discuss a little of what they had endured. Some things she still wasn't ready to talk about.

"I'm sorry, Tristan," she said, surprising them both.

Cree could admit to not being one who apologized often, but he deserved an apology.

"I'm sorry I put us through that. Looking back, I wish I would've taken a beat before reacting. There are so many things I regret about that time, but... I was hurt by your decision and how you didn't tell me you were considering a new agent. Yes, I understand why you went with Ralph, but..."

As flashes of that night and their heated argument came to the forefront of her mind, a sudden bout of emotion gripped her. She had lost a part of herself that night, and her self-confidence had taken a major hit. She'd only been twenty-four, newly graduated from law school and had put her heart and soul into starting her sports agency. When Triston shoved her aside for a new agent, it had crushed her.

Unexpected tears filled Cree's eyes, and a tightness gripped her throat.

What the hell?

She swallowed hard and blinked rapidly, trying to keep the unwanted tears at bay. She wasn't a crier, but this subject always hit her right in the feels. Actually, anything involving Tristan always had a visceral effect on her, and when they broke up...

"We were supposed to be a team," she continued, her words coming out on a sob. "Ride or die, we were supposed to be together forever. It was going to be you and me against everyone else, and we were going to be unstoppable. You on the field and me with my sports agency."

Cree startled when Tristan's large hand covered hers on top of the table. "Baby, I am so sorry," he whispered.

He brought her hand to his lips and placed a kiss on the inside of her palm.

"If I could go back and make different choices I would. I would've fought harder for us, and I sure as hell wouldn't have signed with Ralph before talking it through with you. But everything moved so quickly. One minute he and I were just having conversations and the next I was a client.

"I swear to you, Cree, all the while he talked to me about

what he could do for my career, I kept thinking you and I would be set for life. All our plans and dreams would come to fruition, and we'd live happily ever after."

Cree didn't miss the sincerity in his eyes or the emotion in his tone. They were so damn young back then. Kids trying to be grown and deal with grown folk's stuff. They'd been in way over their heads, and their decisions and how they'd handled the situation reflected that.

If only she had stopped a moment to listen to him, to give him a chance to explain, there wouldn't have been so much heartache for both of them.

"I still have the check you sent back to me," Tristan said quietly before squeezing and releasing her hand. He returned his attention to his plate, picking at the food. "I knew you were still mad when it was returned to me. Then months later, after I finally signed the divorce papers, I found out you had closed your agency."

After he had moved to Philly and played in his first few games, he had sent her a check for a hundred thousand dollars. She wasn't sure what had shocked her the most, the check amount or the note that had come with it.

You'll always be mine, and all I want to do is love and take care of you. Please let me. I miss you.

The money would've been enough to keep her agency open, but her ego got in the way. She had made a rash decision and closed the agency. Despite dreaming of having one since she was a kid, after her breakup with Tristan, she hadn't wanted anything to do with professional athletes.

All I want to do is love and take care of you. Please let me.

The words from the letter played on loop in her mind and tears pricked her eyes. Walking away from Tristan had been a mistake. Though her anger had always been directed at him, their breakup had been her fault. She was the one who had reacted before thinking and ruined everything.

"Damn, baby. You know I can't handle your tears," Tristan said softly.

He reached over and rubbed her arm, and his gentleness only made her stupid tears fall faster. Cree couldn't seem to make them stop, which only pissed her off. She wasn't a damn crybaby, and she was horrified that she was silently bawling in public.

As she dabbed at her face with one of the napkins the server had left with the food, Tristan stood. He pulled out his wallet and dropped enough money on the table to cover the meals for everyone in the restaurant. Then he tugged her out of her seat and into his arms.

"Everything is going to be okay," he whispered, and placed a lingering kiss against her temple. "Come on. Let's go."

Keeping his strong arm around her, he guided her through the small restaurant. No one was probably paying her any mind, but Cree kept her eyes lowered, refusing to look at anyone. She just needed to get out of there so she could pull herself together.

The moment they were outside, she inhaled a long breath before releasing it slowly. Neither of them spoke as they walked to Tristan's car. When she was settled into the vehicle, she used the heel of her palm to dab at a few rogue tears that crept down her cheeks. She hated crying and couldn't remember the last time she'd shed a tear.

Tristan climbed into the car and pulled out of the parking lot without saying anything. He just reached over and held her hand and drove.

Cree appreciated the quietness in the car. She didn't want to talk, and she didn't care where they went, as long as they were together.

Chapter Sixteen

Tristan thought for sure Cree would protest when he brought her back to his place. She didn't. As a matter of fact, except to ask for water, she hadn't said much since they arrived. Which concerned him. The woman was combative on any given day, which was part of her charm. But a quiet, sullen Cree was uncomfortable.

For the last thirty minutes, they'd been sitting on his sofa listening to Maxwell's smooth, melodic voice pouring through the surround-sound speakers. He was currently singing about a temporary night for two. The R & B heartthrob, as Cree once described him, was her favorite singer, and Tristan hoped hearing his music would help relax her.

At least she had made herself comfortable. Shortly after they arrived, she took off her jacket and slipped off her tall boots. That left her in a white button-down blouse and a fitted brown skirt that stopped just above her knees.

Tristan smiled when he glanced down at her sock-covered feet. Her brown football pattern socks weren't a surprise considering how much she loved the sport.

"I see your sock game is still on point," he said, and she snorted but didn't comment.

One of the many things that drew him to her when they were younger was that she was a sports fan. Cree was the only woman he knew who enjoyed every sport but especially football and basketball. They'd had their share of arguments over both, and it used to turn him on when she spouted team and player stats.

She'd been in her early twenties at the time, and he didn't doubt she was an even bigger sports fan now. Had she watched any of his games? Attended any of them in person? And if she did, she probably critiqued every one of his plays, good and bad.

The thought made him smile, but then another thought popped into his mind. It was because of him she no longer had her sports agency, and he needed to make things right in that area. She had probably only gone into entertainment law because he destroyed her dream.

Yeah, he'd make things right but now wasn't the best time to bring up the subject. The last thing he wanted to do was drum up more bad memories. He just hoped she'd consider becoming an agent again because she was great at it. He wanted another chance to help her build her business. Now he had the means to assist her in more ways than one, including finding athletes she could represent.

Tristan released a quiet sigh, debating on what to say next. Having her this close, feeling her curves against him while inhaling her fragrance made it hard to focus on a bigger issue. Her tears from earlier. Cree was too stubborn to cry. At least that's how she was back in the day, and that hadn't changed.

So, what were the tears really about? Because he didn't think she was crying about the argument they'd had that night so many years ago. No, it had to be something else causing her sadness, but what?

Or maybe he was reading too much into this. He could admit their breakup almost destroyed him mentally and emotionally. He'd been a wreck, but the intense workouts and playing football helped redirect his focus. Though Cree was never far from his thoughts, thanks to the sport he loved, he had finally been able to move on with his life. And from what he could see, she had too.

He tightened his arm around Cree and rested his chin on top of her head. "Where do we go from here?" he asked. "Because walking away from you is not an option. I'm here to stay."

She was silent for so long, Tristan didn't think she'd respond.

"I think we owe it to ourselves to give us a second chance," she said, her voice was quiet but strong.

His heart leaped. She was surprising him for the second time that day.

"Moments like right now," Cree continued, "remind me of how things used to be between us, especially our quiet times. Cuddled on the sofa next to you feels as natural as breathing."

"I agree," Tristan said, and kissed the side of her forehead. "It's probably because my feelings for you haven't changed. Just because we weren't together doesn't mean you don't still own my heart."

She grunted and shook her head. "And it sounds like you're still the sweet talker I fell in lo—"

Her words stopped abruptly, and Tristan smiled. She still cared about him, and she was attracted to him as much as he was to her. That was good, but she probably had no idea the real effect she had on him. Not just what her nearness did to his body physically, but how she made his pulse amp with just a look. Or how his heart melted when they shared a memory of years past. Cree meant the world to him, and he'd give up his wealth if it meant having her as his wife again.

Until then, it was great knowing the intense connection he'd felt at her office that first day hadn't been one-sided. Otherwise, she wouldn't have signed him. The money she stood to make for herself and for the law firm wouldn't have stopped her from saying "no" to representing him. If she'd hated him so much, no way would she be anywhere near him. That he knew for a fact, and it was all the encouragement he needed to continue pursuing her.

She turned in his arms and searched his eyes before her gaze went to his lips. Desire, that had been stirring within him since running into her outside the spa, flared to life. He wanted to kiss her. Hell, he wanted to do so much more than kiss, but he didn't want to take advantage while she was vulnerable.

He'd follow her lead. Give her whatever she wanted or needed from him.

He cupped her cheek and caressed her soft skin with the pad of his thumb. He was still struggling with the fact that she was even there. That she was allowing him to hold her close like this.

God, he missed her. He missed this. Missed the quiet moments they used to share. There'd been times where they easily tuned out the world around them, as if it was just the two of them and no one else existed. He wanted that again.

Cree lifted her hand and ran her palm over the scruff on his face. "I like this look on you, but I don't like that it hides your dimples," she said quietly, and Triston smiled.

"I can go and shave right now if you want me to."

She gave him a small smile, but there was still sadness in her pretty brown eyes. A lone tear hung from her long eyelash, and Tristan wanted to erase all that ailed her.

"Shaving is not necessary. What I want is for you to kiss me."

Tristan's heart rattled inside his chest. "There's nothing I wouldn't do for you, Cree," he said as he lowered his head and covered her mouth with his.

He nibbled on her top lip and then her lower lip, but the way they were sitting made kissing a little awkward. They must've been thinking the same thing because Cree lifted up, then sat on his lap, and looped her arms around his neck.

He held her tightly as he loved on her mouth. With each lap of his tongue, he hoped she could feel how much he cared about her. How much he needed her. They were made for each other. Meant to be together like peanut butter and jelly, and he would never let her walk out of his life again. He wouldn't be able to handle it a second time.

Cree relaxed in his arms as their lips and tongues got reacquainted. She tasted of wine and something savory, and he could kiss her all day, but it still wouldn't be enough. He missed this, and the longer he kissed her, the more he wanted what they'd lost.

As he deepened their connection, her hand moved to the back of his head, holding him in place as if making sure he didn't pull away. As if that would happen. No way she was ever getting rid of him.

His hand glided down her side, relishing in every dip and curve of her body until he came to her firm ass. Tristan squeezed. She moaned. And he hummed against her sweet lips. Her breasts were pressed against his chest, and arousal pulsed through his body. He wanted to touch her, every inch of her, and he wanted to do it without the barrier of their clothing.

Kissing and caressing her was nice, but he needed to feel all of her.

One of her hands moved to his face, and she cupped his cheek just before breaking their kiss.

"I'm ready for that tour you offered the other day, but let's start with your bedroom," she said, her voice rough with desire.

Tristan's heart rate kicked up as he searched her eyes. He was reading her loud and clear. Yeah, he wanted to show her his bedroom and so much more, but once they crossed this line, there was no going back.

"Cree, are you sure? If I show you my bedroom, a room no other woman has been in, then you're mine."

She swallowed hard, but her gaze didn't waver. "I'm sure."

Without another word, Tristan leaned forward, and Cree started to move out of his arms.

"Hold on," he said. After a slight adjustment, he cradled her in his arms and stood.

Carrying her across the living room and down the hallway, he headed to his bedroom, half expecting her to say *wait*. He thought she'd tell him that she'd made a mistake, that this was not what she wanted. She didn't. Her arms were securely around his neck as she kissed him.

This was happening.

Tristan wasn't used to being vulnerable, but when it came to Cree, he was afraid to hope. Afraid that one wrong move or a misunderstood comment would send her running again. He didn't just want her back in his life, he needed her. She was the puzzle piece missing in his world, and he wouldn't be complete until he knew she was back for good.

He entered the bedroom and carefully set her on her feet. Before he could step back, Cree's warm, soft hands slid beneath his shirt, and her palms glided up his body, then stopped at his pecs. Unable to help himself, Tristan made them jump beneath her touch, and she laughed.

Her eyes glittered with mischief, and she was smiling for the first time since leaving the restaurant. "Impressive," she said.

He wrapped his arms around her and pulled her close. "Oh, baby. You haven't seen nothing yet."

Chapter Seventeen

Cree's heart was practically beating out of her chest as Tristan took his time unbuttoning her shirt, while at the same time he grazed his lips along the length of her neck, kissing and sucking. No doubt leaving a few love marks along the way.

How he managed to multi-task with such precision was a mystery to her, but she loved it. She loved everything about this moment, and she knew when they finally came together, it would be good. Better than good. Tristan never did anything half-ass, and she doubted that had changed.

Squirming under his touch, feeling his heat radiating off him, she fumbled with his belt buckle as if she had never unfastened one before. The man had her breathing erratically, her hands shaking, and her pulse pounding in her ears, and they hadn't even made it to the bed yet.

When Tristan finished with her shirt, he started sliding it down her arms, then tossed it to the floor. All the while his lips caressed her cheek, then worked their way down to the pulsing hollow at the base of her throat, and he continued to her shoulders, peppering kisses against her skin.

Cree was on fire. She was burning up everywhere he touched causing heat to soar through her veins like a match, igniting a flame through her body.

It was already clear he planned to take his time, but her impatience had her squirming against him. As if sensing she was about ready to leap out of her skin, Tristan's strong arm went around her waist, and he crushed her to him. His lips met hers in a searing kiss that had her about ready to lose her mind.

He had always been wickedly skilled with his mouth, and that hadn't changed either. The man already had her moaning in pleasure, silently begging for more as their kiss built in its intensity.

"Oh yes," she murmured against his mouth.

She cupped his face between her hands and deepened their connection while delighting on every lap of his tongue. Her chest heaved. Her heart beat double-timed, and her self-control was quickly dwindling. She wanted them naked and in bed, and though she loved a little foreplay as much as the next person, she couldn't take much more.

Tristan might not be in a hurry, but her body was vibrating with desire, and she was tempted to take matters into her own hands. She needed him to touch her everywhere, then make her come over and over again... like now.

She jerked her mouth from his, her breaths coming in short spurts. "Take your clothes off," she said and reached for the zipper on the side of her hip to undo her skirt but stopped when she realized Tristan wasn't moving.

"What?" she said. "I've been waiting a long time to be intimate with you again, and I want you... now. Hurry up."

His low chuckle filled the quietness in the room, and Cree

lowered her head to hide her smile. She tugged down the zipper of her skirt, letting the garment puddle around her ankles. Next went her socks, leaving her in a white lace bra and pantie set.

"Still as bossy as hell, but I wouldn't have you any other way," Tristan said, and when Cree looked up, the only thing that remained on him were gray boxer briefs.

Have. Mercy.

He stood before her like a Nubian god with rippling muscles everywhere she looked. The elaborate tattoos she had spied on his arms days ago stood out even more, and they blended well with his bad boy physique. From his biceps and his muscular chest down to his washboard abs, the man was perfection.

As her attention went lower, she squeezed her legs together to help tamp down the throbbing pulse between her thighs. He definitely knew how to fill a pair of briefs, and his thick erection wanted out.

"Damn, baby. I didn't think you could get any sexier," Tristan said, speaking the exact words she was thinking about him. He moved closer and ran the back of his fingers over the lace on her bra. "But clearly I was wrong."

Without another word, he bent slightly and gripped the back of her thighs and lifted her into the air. Cree couldn't stop herself from laughing. The man was ridiculously strong, and he held her as if she was weightless.

When he didn't immediately lay her on the bed, she wrapped her arms around his neck and her legs around his waist. Then she kissed him. They kissed like they couldn't get enough, and the hunger with every lap of his tongue had her thoughts spinning.

There were moments like now that she found it hard to believe she and Tristan were back in each other's lives. It just didn't seem real. It was like a fantasy come to life, and she wanted to experience it all. The kisses. The touches. The heavy breathing. The sweaty sex. She wanted it all.

By the time Tristan finally laid her on the bed, Cree knew it wouldn't take much to make her come. She was already panting as she watched him remove a condom from his wallet and set the foil packet next to the pillow.

Cree made quick work of removing her bra and tossing it to the floor. Next, she scurried out of her panties and let them join the rest of her clothes, all before Tristan climbed onto the bed next to her.

"I want you inside of me," she said breathlessly. He already had her so turned on she was struggling to get air into her lungs.

"I will—when I'm ready," he said casually as his heated gaze traveled the length of her body from head to toe. "Damn," he said, drawing out the word as he eased onto the bed without taking his eyes off her.

Cree reached for him, but Tristan wasn't having it. He gathered her hands together and held them over her head, then smiled down at her, not caring that she was squirming.

"Clearly, some things haven't changed. I didn't let you rush me back then, and I sure as hell don't plan on you rushing me now. Not when I haven't had you in years. It's been way too long, baby, and I'm taking my time getting reacquainted with what's always been mine."

And that's what he did, he kissed her senseless while holding her wrists over head with one hand, while his other glided sensually down the center of her body. Cree bucked against his scorching touch, whimpering his name.

When his hand reached the apex between her thighs, he teased her with his fingers, gliding them in and out of her wetness before his mouth took their place.

"Oh my God," she cried out, fisting the sheets on each side of her while he did wicked things to her.

Touching her, tasting her, he not only pushed her to the edge, but she felt as if she had tumbled over a cliff when her release rocked her to the core. Cree rode the waves of ecstasy until she could barely see straight.

Ohmigod. Ohmigod. Ohmigod, she panted, struggling to catch her breath.

Her irregular breathing didn't phase Tristan. At some point, he had shed his boxer brief and wasted no time sheathing himself. But not before Cree got a view of his impressive dick. The man was hung like a horse, and she couldn't wait to ride him before the night was over.

But right now, he had other plans as he moved his large body between her thighs. "So that we're clear," he said close to her mouth, "you're mine." Then his demanding kiss left no room for discussion as his mouth moved over hers. Pleasure radiated through her body as her emotions whirled, and her thoughts spun out of control.

As their tongues tangled, the head of his dick bumped against her opening, sending excitement racing through Cree's veins. At this rate, she was prepared to agree to anything, especially when he slid into her, stretching her ever so gently as her body adjusted around him.

Oh yes. Yes. Yes. Yes! Her mind screamed as Tristan moved inside of her, reminding her how amazing they used to be together. It didn't take long for her to catch his rhythm, and they moved in perfect sync.

He reached between them without missing a beat, and when the pad of his thumb made contact with her clit, Cree almost lost it. Her hips bucked against him as he drove into her, picking up speed with each thrust. But she wanted to feel even more of him.

The moment she wrapped her legs around his waist, his hand moved from between their bodies and he growled.

Bracing both hands on the bed on either side of her head, his thrusts grew more demanding.

"Cree," he ground out, and as expected, he drove into her like a madman.

He loved when her legs were around his waist, but he also hated the position because she drew him in deeper. She loved the feel of him filling her completely, but he usually lost control sooner than he preferred.

Passion rippled through her with each stroke, and as their bodies picked up speed, Tristan drove into her harder.

Feeling her release nearing, Cree's fingers dug into the back of his shoulders as he drove into her faster. On the next thrust, she lost it. Her interior muscles gripped him tightly, and she screamed his name over and over as she rode out her release.

"Cree! Ahh, yessss!" Tristan growled before he collapsed on top of her.

With her arms wrapped around him, Cree held on to him while their erratic breathing filled the quietness in the room. They stayed locked together that way until they caught their breaths.

No words were spoken. None were needed as they basked in the aftermath of their lovemaking.

Chapter Eighteen

Cree lay on her back, her heart finally beating normally. Sex with Tristan had always been exciting because he was a thorough lover. He knew what she liked, what turned her on, and what moves always sent her over the edge of her control.

Today, though, their chemistry in the bedroom had been on a whole different level. Maybe because they were older. Or maybe it felt unbelievably wonderful because it had been a long time since she'd been with a man. Or maybe it was because she was still in love with Tristan—something she was finally ready to admit to herself.

Whatever it was, she would never get enough of him.

Tristan had renewed something within her that she thought long dead. Desire. Passion. Love. Cree had forgotten what it was like to make love with a man who truly cared about her. Someone who reached down into her soul and loved on every part of her body and her mind if that were possible.

Hooking back up with Tristan again wasn't the mistake she thought it would be, but instead, it was an opportunity for them to try again. A second chance for their relationship, and Cree could admit to wanting that, even if it scared her a little.

But what would that look like exactly? Maybe they could just play it by ear and see what happened.

When the bathroom door opened, Cree glanced across the room as Tristan moved toward the bed in all his naked glory. Her heartbeat picked up speed with every step he took, and she couldn't look away. The man's body was something to behold. Every inch of his muscular form was carved to perfection from his defined arms, solid chest, on down to the magnificent tool between his legs. Seeing his semi-erect shaft reminded her of all they'd done in the last hour, and what she knew he was capable of doing.

Cree placed her hand on her chest as if that would help get her heartbeat back to a normal rhythm. The man was absolutely breathtaking.

"You keep looking at me like that, I'm going to insist on another round between the sheets with you," he said as he climbed back into bed and under the covers.

"I'm counting on it," she said seriously. She hadn't had nearly enough of him.

"Let's talk about what happened at the restaurant," Tristan said as he wrapped his strong arm around her and pulled her against his side.

"Let's not." Cree rested her head on his hard chest and sighed.

Tristan had always been in touch with his emotions and hers as well. He also used to be a good communicator, except the one time that had sent their relationship imploding in every direction. Maybe that was why learning he had signed with another agent had hurt so much. He hadn't talked about it at all and then *bam!* The news fell on her like a two-ton bolder, and she hadn't handled it well. There'd been more going on at the time, and that hadn't helped the situation.

So, the last thing she wanted was to rehash that subject all over again. "Tristan, I'm sorry about what happened at the restaurant. The tears caught me off guard too. It's clear the breakup was hard on us both, and you were right, we were so young back then. There were things we both should've done differently."

He kissed the top of her head. "Yeah, I have a lot of regrets, but I hope you can forgive me, Cree. You have to know I would never intentionally hurt you."

"I know, and I knew back then, but..." She shook her head. "Anyway, I forgive you. I forgive us. Now can we leave the past in the past and move on from here?"

"Definitely," he said without hesitation. "But I have a question for you."

She tweaked his nipple and smiled when he hissed. "Of course, you do because you know how much I love being questioned," she said sarcastically.

He chuckled. "Yeah, I know, but this is important."

Recognizing the seriousness in his tone, she said, "Okay, what's the question?"

"Have you ever considered restarting your sports agency?"

Surprised, Cree wondered if he could now read minds. She'd been thinking about her agency a lot over the last couple of weeks. Partly because he was back in her life, and it was impossible to be around him and not to think of the agency. He'd been a key part of the success of it—and the downfall of it —but she'd come to terms with that not being his fault.

"Yes. As a matter of fact, I have," she said and went on to tell him that, even if she didn't restart her agency, she was seriously thinking about opening her own law firm. Things still weren't great between her and Warren.

"Do you think Warren could be jealous of your success?" Tristan asked. "Which would be crazy. If you're successful, that spills over into the firm. Meaning he reaps the benefits one way or another. He should be trying to support whatever is working for you."

"I agree, but for the last few months, there's been tension between us, and to be honest, I think it is jealousy. He's been bringing in clients, but his billable hours are nowhere near mine."

She gave Tristan examples of some of their encounters, including the one from a couple of weeks ago. For the most part, Warren had been keeping his distance, but every now and then, he'd say something in a meeting or in passing that was condescending or just mean.

Cree leaned back and glanced at Tristan. "Why are you asking about the agency?"

He released a long yawn as he tightened his arms around her.

"I've just been thinking. Actually, I've thought about this a lot over the years, but more so since moving back to Chicago. I hate that you closed your sports agency, and I feel responsible."

He explained how she'd been an amazing agent, even when she was still learning the industry. With her love for sports, her experience, and her ability to negotiate great deals, he wanted her to try rebuilding her agency.

Cree's heart swelled hearing him talk about her accomplishments and how impressed he'd always been with her natural abilities to lead and make things happen. As he told her about the potential office space, excitement swirled inside of Cree. The more he talked, the more the idea of reopening her agency appealed to her. It would be a dream come true considering she'd always wanted to be a sports agent.

"I'm going to seriously think about it," she said, resting her head back on his solid chest.

Leaving Ellis, Priestly, and Watts wouldn't be easy because she liked her job and most of the people she worked with. But to have her own firm or agency appealed to her entrepreneurial spirit.

"Now, let's talk about us," Tristan said, and Cree had to stop herself from groaning.

Why couldn't he just go with the flow instead of needing to spell everything out? She almost laughed because this was how things had gone the last time they were together. He wanted it clear about where they stood while she just wanted to have a good time.

"We're not kids anymore," he continued. "And I want you back in my life."

"You have me back in your life. Otherwise, I wouldn't be lounging in your bed."

"I want more, Cree," he said, no humor in his tone. "I want a commitment."

She lifted her head and narrowed her eyes at him. "What type of commitment?"

"I want us to pick up where we left off. I want you to be my woman. I want to be introduced as your man. Not your friend. Not your client. No more hiding me from your friends and family."

Cree huffed out a breath. "Tristan, why can't we just hang out, have fun? We're getting reacquainted. Why do we have to put a label on—"

"Cree, I'm not going to be your dirty little secret anymore. I stood for that shit back in the day. Not this time. We're either all in or nothing. Meaning, we date like normal people and meet each other's friends and family and build from there. I was serious about wanting my wife back.

I love you. I never stopped loving you," he said with conviction.

She loved him too, but she wasn't ready to say the words. Not yet, and that didn't mean she'd never say them. But she was still getting used to the idea of them being together. Could she ever see herself marrying him again? Yes, but not until she knew for sure they'd stay married next time.

"We can take it slow if you want, Cree, but just know you still own my heart. I want what we once had and more.

"While I was recovering from injuries, I realized just how short life is. How things can change in a heartbeat. I had big plans for my career, and I know for a fact that, just because we plan out our lives, doesn't mean that's the way it'll turn out. I'm not taking anything for granted anymore. I know you and I are meant to be together, that we still more than care about each other, and I want us to build on that."

Cree pulled out of his hold and returned her attention to the ceiling while trying not to growl her frustration. After such an incredible afternoon, the last thing she wanted to do was argue. She understood Tristan's demand, and he was right, to a point. He was the love of her life all those years ago. Yet, she'd kept their relationship a secret, which hadn't been fair to him.

Still, she'd had good reason for keeping things quiet the last time and would have just as good a reason this time around. Like before, Cree was the one whose integrity was at stake when it came to her career. Except this time, she had options. She had money. She had an incredible track record as a kick-ass attorney, and she wasn't just starting out with a new business.

"All or nothing, Cree," Tristan said when she glanced at him, and by the serious expression on his face and in his tone, he wouldn't settle for anything less than a yes.

It was more than just her career she needed to protect, though. She had to protect her heart too. What if she jumped all in and they broke up again? The first time almost killed her. No way she could go through that again.

But we deserve a second chance, a small voice in the back of her mind said. *And he's worth the risk.*

Her cell phone, which she had brought into the room earlier, vibrated on the nightstand. That was twice in the last few minutes. When she glanced at the screen, there were several missed text messages. One from her mother, another from Dorian, and a couple from her father.

She skimmed Dorian's first since it had come through over an hour ago.

Come to Mom and Dad's at your own risk. Mom is in match-making mode. She invited that pastor to come over later... for you.

Cree shook her head. Would her mother ever quit with her schemes? Cree skipped her mom's message and glanced at the ones from her dad. After reading them, she groaned.

"What is it?" Tristan said from over her shoulder.

"I forgot I told my dad I would come by and read over some legal documents today. I was supposed to be there hours ago."

Cree skimmed her mother's text, which was asking if she was still able to stop by and read over the documents. She also told her that there would be dinner for her.

Hopefully, her mother's guest would be long gone by now, but maybe not.

Cree set her phone down and turned to Tristan. "Do you have plans for the evening?"

"No, why?"

"Well, since you're *my man,* I guess there's no better time than the present to meet my parents. But I should probably warn you about my mother."

His brows dipped into a frown. "Why? Does she have six

fingers on one hand or something? Or is she going to interrogate me, then send me away crying?"

"No, worse. She planned to introduce me to the youth pastor at her church, and I have a feeling that he might be at their house."

Tristan shrugged. "No big deal. We'll just explain that you're taken. I'm sure she'll be fine with that once she meets me. She's going to love me."

Cree snorted. "Ha! If I were you, I wouldn't be so sure about that."

Chapter Nineteen

Tristan followed Cree's direction to her parents' bed and breakfast while thinking that this had been an amazing day so far. Though he had dreamed about him and Cree reconnecting someday, his imagination hadn't done the reality justice. He fell more in love with her with every moment he spent with her, and he was more confident than ever that they belonged together.

As he parked a few doors up from her parents' bed and breakfast, Cree said, "It looks like my brother, Zion and my Uncle Idris, my dad's twin brother, are here." She pointed out their vehicles.

"Anything I should know before we go inside?"

"Only that the guys will probably be glued to their seats with a beer in hand watching football. Oh, and my dad's twin, who some call the bad boy and black sheep in the family, is opposite of my dad in almost every way. Not only is he rough around the edges, but he's been married and divorced three times with three sets of kids. Surprisingly, they all get along and are the epitome of a blended family.

"My mom and my Aunt GiGi are also here. Aunt GiGi helps with the business, especially on weekends and during the busy seasons. Oh, and since you're a tall, good-looking man," Cree said smiling, and Tristan chuckled, "she'll probably have you blushing before the evening is over. As for my mom, she's a wild card. I never know what she's going to say or do. If she really is on one of her matchmaking kicks as my sister claims, there might be some random guy inside."

"I'm not worried. One look at me, and your mom's going to kick him out. I'm irresistible," Tristan assured her.

Cree snorted. "Yeah, we'll see, Mr. Irresistible. My mother is not easy to please. Then again, if you flash those damn dimples at her, you might win her over."

As they approached the three-story Greystone, Tristan admired the exterior of the bed and breakfast. On the ride over, Cree had given him a little history on it, while also telling him that her parents had both worked in corporate America. When they got tired of the high-pressure and long hours, they quit their jobs and opened the B & B.

The Italian architectural style exterior was even more impressive than he had imagined. If the interior was just as nice, it was no wonder the place had been featured in various magazines. According to Cree, the seven-bedroom suites were always booked up during the peak season, which included spring, summer, and the end of the year holidays.

Instead of going to the bed and breakfast, they walked along a path on the side of the building that led to her parents' cottage in back. Once they reached the door, Cree rang the doorbell, and a few minutes later, the door swung open. An older man appeared, but his attention was on something behind him.

"Hey, sweetheart," the man said absently while looking over his shoulder. "Come on..."

145

The sound of cheering came from somewhere behind him, and he rushed back into the house.

"*O—kay*. That was my father." Cree chuckled. "Clearly, we arrived during an important play." She pushed the door open for them to enter. "That's the risk of showing up in the middle of a football game, especially when Chicago is playing. He's a huge fan."

"Totally understandable," Tristan said as they moved past the foyer and stood on the edge of a living room.

Besides her father, who was standing near the large television mounted on the wall, there were two other guys. The one who looked exactly like her father must've been her uncle, and the other had to be her brother Zion.

"Hey, you guys," Cree said loud enough to get their attention.

"I was wondering if you had forgotten about stopping by," Cree's father said, his attention still on the television screen. "I'll get those papers for you right after this play."

Tristan chuckled and moved closer. "Who's winning?"

"Chicago is up by..." Zion said but stopped and jerked his head around, clearly surprised to hear a man's voice. He did a double take, and Tristan laughed at his comical expression.

"That knucklehead is my brother, Zion," Cree said from next to Tristan, a smirk on her face.

"Hold up." Zion bolted out of his seat, and that got their father and uncle's attention. "Tristan Whitmore?" Zion said in awe, and Tristan laughed.

"*Whaaat?*" Cree's uncle said, fully turning around in his seat.

Tristan knew he and Cree's father were identical twins, but it was wild to see them next to each other looking exactly alike.

"Well, I'll be damn," Uncle Idris said. "It is him, but his ass should be on somebody's football field playing. Not standing in this living room and wasting all that talent."

Tristan grunted, hating to be reminded of what he'd been through the last nine months. "I'd love to be out there playing, but I guess there are just some things we have no control over."

"Knock it off, Idris," Cree's father jumped into the conversation and shook Tristan's hand. "Don't pay my brother any mind. He always speaks before thinking, and sorry for not seeing you when I opened the door. I was a little distracted. I'm Israel. It's nice to meet you."

"Nice to meet you too, sir."

"Man, it's a pleasure," Zion said and shook Tristan's hand. "What brings you to town?"

Tristan reached for Cree's hand. Though he had told her that he wanted them to go public with their relationship, she hadn't sounded too convinced. This would be the test.

Interlocking their fingers, he gently tugged her forward until she was standing beside him. Then he brought the back of her hand to his lips. "I grew up here, but what has me staying for good is your sister."

Cree looked at him with a shy smile that was so not like her, but it was adorable to see vulnerability in her eyes.

She turned her attention to the men in her family. "Tristan and I are a couple."

* * *

Cree cleared her throat. It seemed so foreign to introduce her family to a boyfriend, and not just any boyfriend, but the man she was in love with. The last time she brought anyone home to meet her parents was senior prom, and the only reason she'd done it then was because her father insisted.

Now here she was, her nerves on edge as three of the most important men in her life looked at her in surprise.

Zion crossed his arms and grinned. The former cop turned security specialist had always tried playing a big brother role with his four sisters. He didn't seem to care that he was actually the baby in the family, and right now, she was fairly sure he was about to say something stupid.

"Well, well, well, somebody finally landed my stubborn, hard-to-get-along-with, take no bullshit, sister. Tristan, man, I hope you know what you're getting into."

Cree punched her brother in the arm. "Shut up."

"Ow! Damn, Cree."

"Language, boy," their father said to Zion, then turned his gaze to Tristan. "I guess that means we'll be seeing you around here often. Good. I look forward to getting to know you."

"What my brother means is, you fuck around and hurt her, you'll be dealing with us," her Uncle Idris said while hiking up his pants, the ones being held up by old suspenders. "I don't give a damn who you are or how fast you can run. I don't even care how many MVPs you have or how many NFL records you've broken. I also don't care how many millions you have in the bank. Hurt my niece, and I'll hunt you down and kick your ass."

Her uncle said all that with a straight face, then dropped down into his seat and picked up his beer.

Cree bit the inside of her cheek, trying not to laugh, but when she glanced at Tristan, and the way his eyebrows almost reached his scalp, she burst out laughing. Tristan and Zion joined in, but their father just frowned and shook his head.

"Like I said, Tristan, don't pay my brother any attention."

Zion snorted. "Uncle Idris isn't the one he should be worried about. Cree chew men up and spit them out before they even know what happened."

A twinge of guilt pierced Cree in the chest at the truth in those words. Hadn't she done just that to Tristan years ago? What was to keep her from reacting before thinking the next time they had a disagreement? Because she knew there'd be a next time. That's how she was wired. Fight first and ask questions later.

Tristan slipped his arm around her and placed a kiss against her temple. "I'm not worried. Cree's it for me, and I'm not going anywhere," he said as if reading her mind.

God, this man. He really was perfect for her, and if anyone could put up with her prickliness, it was Tristan.

"Glad to hear that," her father said, nodding in approval. "Grab a seat, young man, and watch the rest of the game with us. Want a beer?"

"Sure. That would be great," Tristan said, and when Cree's father started for the kitchen, she stopped him.

"I'll get it, Dad."

While in the kitchen, Cree's heart swelled as conversation between the men flowed easily. They pulled Tristan into their group as if knowing him forever, and it didn't take long for trash talking to start as they tuned back into the game.

A roar of laughter boomed through the house, and Cree smiled. Why had she been so worried to introduce Tristan to the family? Anyone who spent time with him learned quickly that he was one of the good guys. The man could charm the grumpiest person, but more than that, he genuinely loved people.

In hindsight, Cree wished she had introduced him to her family years ago, even before she married him. Maybe then she would've thought twice about walking away from Tristan. Instead, there'd only been Essence to tell her that she was being too rash. That she shouldn't divorce her husband after one disagreement.

Since no one else in her family knew about her and Tristan, there'd been no one, like her dad, to tell her to take a breath before making a life-altering decision. He had often been her confident, gently guiding her with his quiet strength and wisdom.

But not then. Not when she'd needed him the most. All because she hadn't let anyone in. She had kept her business to herself.

So, when her marriage ended and her life crumbled around her, Dad hadn't been there for her. He hadn't been able to tell her that she shouldn't walk away from the man she loved, especially without a fight. He couldn't hold her in his comforting arms and tell her that everything would be okay. All because he hadn't known her world had fallen apart.

"You and Tristan Whitmore, huh?"

So caught up in her thoughts, Cree hadn't heard Zion enter. "Yes," she said absently and set the beers on the counter.

Her little brother, who wasn't all that little at over six feet tall and two hundred pounds, had truly matured over the last few months. It was cool watching him grow into the role of loving husband and father. Not only had he married the mother of his children, twins he hadn't known about until recently, but he gave up his job as a cop. Wanting something safer, he changed careers to become a security specialist with a company that provided personal protection to the rich and famous.

"How'd you and Tristan meet? How long have you been dating? I'm shocked the news hasn't made it to the media, especially since reporters were hounding him like crazy during his recovery. At least before he announced his retirement."

Cree sighed. Sometimes she forgot Tristan used to be in the public's eye. She debated on how much to share with her brother. Since she and Tristan had talked about what to tell people, she'd just stick with that.

"We met years ago. I was his agent and got him his first NFL contract."

Cree's chest puffed out at that admission. She'd been so busy thinking about Tristan's betrayal and how their marriage ended, she hadn't thought much about how she'd been the catalyst for getting him into the NFL. She had kick-started his professional career, and that was something to be proud of.

Zion's mouth hung open and his eyes were wide. "Seriously? Wow, sis, that's amazing. I had no idea you even knew the guy, let alone represented him at some point in his career."

Cree nodded, hoping the conversation would stop there, but of course it didn't.

"How long were you his agent? Wait, I thought he'd been with Ralph Dawson his whole career. Why didn't—"

"Stop," Cree said, holding up her hands. "It's a long story, and I'm going to give you the Cliff's Notes version. Tristan started out with me, but I was a new agent at the time, still learning the industry. Ralph came along and took his career further than I ever could."

"You don't know that," Zion said, a frown on his face. "You're the best at everything you set out to do. You could've been just as good as Ralph if not better."

"Thanks for that," she shrugged, "but Ralph did a great job with Tristan's career."

To think, a couple of weeks ago, she wouldn't have admitted that. She'd still been calling foul on how everything had played out back then. Now, she was comfortable giving credit where credit was due.

"Yeah, I guess," Zion said.

Cree didn't bother telling him that she was representing Tristan again. Actually, she wasn't ready to think about that in length. Her moral compass was already tilted, and at some point, she would need to make some decisions. Dating a client, even if Tristan was so much more than that, wasn't a good idea no matter how she tried to spin it in her mind.

Before Zion could ask more questions, their mother's voice could be heard outside and getting closer.

"Oh, boy," Zion said and grabbed the beers, then hustled out of the kitchen.

"Don't leave me," Cree whisper-shouted to his retreating back just as their mother rushed into the house and straight to the kitchen with a picnic basket. She was followed by a man Cree didn't recognize, as well as her Aunt GiGi.

"Hey sweetie, I'm glad you're here," her mother said, setting the basket on the counter, then giving her a quick hug.

Her mother, with deep bronze skin and her straight hair pulled back into a bun, had changed out of her church clothes. She looked comfortable and at home in a long, royal blue and white caftan. Unlike Cree's aunt, her mother's sister, who looked like she'd just left a photoshoot. Like usual, her face was perfectly made up, her long braids freshly done, and she was dressed stylishly in a red sweater dress with a wide belt around her waist.

"I want you to meet the youth pastor from my church," Cree's mom said.

"*Virginia*," Aunt GiGi said in a warning tone. Her aunt rolled her eyes, and Cree smiled, knowing that when Virginia Priestly was on a mission, no one could stop her.

"Pastor Avery, this is my daughter, Cree. The one I was telling you about, and Cree this is Kevin Avery."

Cree shook his hand, and they exchanged pleasantries. The moment was awkward, and the pastor looked as uncomfortable as she felt. He was probably just realizing he was her mother's latest victim of one of many of her matchmaking attempts.

But what was her mom thinking? This guy, though nice looking, was so not Cree's type. He was close to her height with a slim build, and his wire-rimmed glasses gave him a geeky appearance. He looked more like an accountant, who should be sitting behind a desk crunching numbers, than a youth pastor.

Cree wasn't even a little attracted to him. She preferred tall, muscular men who had a bad boy swagger and looked as if he could carry a building on his shoulders. Kind of like her man, the hottie who was currently making his way to the kitchen.

"Whoa. Who's the hunk?" Aunt GiGi gushed and set a grocery bag on the counter. Then she intercepted Tristan before he reached them. "Hi handsome. I'm GiGi, and you are?"

"He's mine, Aunt GiGi. So don't get any ideas," Cree said loud enough for anyone nearby to hear. Then she strolled across the room to save him from her aunt, who attracted men half her age. Cree slid her hand into Tristan's.

"Well, all right, niece. I see you, girl. Seems you have good taste like your auntie."

Cree laughed and made introductions. Her mother didn't say much, but when Tristan greeted her with a kiss to the back of her hand, she giggled like a schoolgirl.

Cree shook her head. Mr. Irresistible strikes again. All she could do was smile as she watched them, including the pastor, fawn over her man. Turns out, the pastor was a huge fan of Tristan's.

Tristan talked to each one of them as if they were the most important people in the world, and Cree fell a little more in love with him. Though her mother and aunt had no clue of his notoriety, Pastor Avery knew more about him than Cree would've thought.

After a few more minutes of conversation, Virginia looped her arm with her guest.

"Pastor Avery, thanks so much for stopping by. I'm glad you were able to have a meal with us at the B & B," she said sweetly as she walked the man to the door. "I know you must get to your next appointment. So, I'm not going to keep you any longer."

He barely had a chance to say goodbye to everyone before her mom practically shoved him out the door.

Cree chuckled. Her mother hadn't mastered the art of being subtle, and clearly, she had changed her mind about him and Cree hooking up.

"Tristan, I hope you're hungry," Virginia said when she strolled back into the kitchen smiling. "Let me fix you a plate, and then we can get to know you better. I want to know your intentions for my daughter."

Cree groaned. *Oh no.*

Chapter Twenty

"I know I said it before, but I'm sorry about my mom and her intrusive questions," Cree said as they strolled down the hallway that led to her condo.

She lived in Hyde Park, a neighborhood in Chicago, and Tristan was looking forward to seeing her living space. Before leaving his place earlier in the day, she had suggested he spend the night with her. Of course, he agreed.

"I had no idea she'd ask about your dating life," Cree continued. "And please don't feel like you have to set up a time for her to meet your family. We're not kids, and she doesn't need to vet the people I associate with. I think she forgets her children are grown, and she's just... she's a lot."

Tristan laughed and gave Cree a kiss on the lips when they stopped in front of her door. "I liked your mom. Hell, I enjoyed the whole family. At least the ones I met today. I'm all for our families getting together because I know my parents would love yours. So no worries, but I will say, when your mom started planning our wedding, I did get a little nervous."

Cree groaned and rested her forehead on his chest. "And

you wondered why I didn't want a big wedding years ago." She lifted her head. "It wasn't just because I was your agent and wanted to keep our nuptials quiet. No, it also had to do with my mother. I know her. She gets an idea in her head and runs with it, which is what she'd do if we ever decided to have a big wedding. Which I don't want by the way."

"Well, when that day comes," and Tristan hoped it would be sooner than later, "we can exchange vows however you want. My number one goal is to make sure my woman is happy."

Tristan backed her against the door before kissing her again. This time, it wasn't just a little peck. This lip-lock was hot, sexy, and a prelude to things to come tonight. They'd touched, hugged, and even stole a few kisses while at her parents' house, and all it did was make him long for more.

When he ended the kiss, Cree was slow to open her eyes, and a sweet smile covered her luscious lips as she did.

"Damn, you're a good kisser," she said before turning to unlock the door. Once inside, she told him to make himself at home, and Tristan planned to.

He glanced around the lavishly decorated space as Cree went about turning on lights. The large, open floor plan gave a view of the high-end kitchen, as well as the dining room and living room to his right. The walls were light gray and covered with colorful, abstract paintings. A white sectional dominated the living room, and a glass table with six, high-back chairs filled the dining area.

After a quick tour of the main floor, they headed upstairs. The three-bedroom, three-bathroom condo was definitely larger than he first realized, and he could see why Cree loved the place.

Tristan followed her into the master bedroom, and the moment he stepped into the room, he inhaled Cree's intoxicating scent. It was one thing to smell the fragrance on her body, but it was a whole different experience to be surrounded by it. The combination of lavender, vanilla, and something spicy drew him farther into the space.

Like the rest of the place, it was beautifully decorated with a gray and white color scheme that captured Cree's personality. Sophisticated. Soft, and the purple, leather headboard with pops of deep purple scattered about the room added a little edginess to the space. It was inviting and made him want to curl up with his woman right after he made mad, passionate love to her.

"I'll be right out," Cree said before entering the ensuite bathroom, closing the door behind her.

Tristan set his duffel bag in the chair near the window and yawned. He couldn't be tired. The night was still young, and he had big plans for his beautiful woman. He was also looking forward to testing out her bed.

He sat on the edge of it and made quick work of getting out of his shoes, socks, shirt, and pants. Which he tossed into the chair with his duffel. That left him in navy blue boxer briefs, but maybe he should lose those too. The way Cree had been flirting with him on the way to her place let him know they both wanted the same thing tonight—each other naked.

Another loud, noisy yawn poured from him, and Tristan dropped back on the bed and stared at the ceiling. What a day. As he thought about the events of the last twelve hours, a smile kicked up the corners of his mouth. It was hard to believe he and Cree had reconciled. They were a couple again, and he was thrilled because deep down he knew they'd make it this time.

Tristan just had to try not to rush everything. He wanted them to remarry, find a house, have a few kids, and then live happily ever after. It wasn't an inconceivable dream, but Cree was not one you could rush. Even if she felt the same as he did, she'd want to take things slow and ease back into their relationship.

As he settled deeper into the comfortable mattress, his eyes drifted closed. All the busyness of the day faded away, and a calmness settled over him. It was as if the quietness, the amazing fragrance in the room, and the bed were lulling him into a state of tranquility that he hadn't felt in a long time.

Yeah, he'd just lie there for a few minutes and soak it all in until...

"Tristan?"

He slowly opened his eyes, then lifted onto his elbows. What he saw had him blinking several times to make sure he wasn't seeing things.

"Wow," he whispered, taking in the angel standing before him. And by angel, he really meant the most alluring supernatural being on this side of heaven.

Was he dreaming? Maybe he had dozed off. Either way, if this was a fantasy, he didn't want to wake up. *Ever*. Playing professional football over the years, he'd been approached by his share of gorgeous women, but no one compared to Cree.

Tristan wanted to just lie there and stare at her—the sexiest woman he'd ever seen. She was standing before him in all white. Literally, dressed like an angel, and she had his dick leaping to attention as he took in the bejeweled bra that barely contained her voluptuous breasts.

The garment as well as the matching panties glittered like diamonds under the bedroom's light, and Tristan couldn't look away. And the garter belt? *Hot damn!* No woman alive wore a garter belt the way she did. And this one, which was also white, held up thigh-high nylons that made her long, shapely legs look even more enticing. The high-heeled shoes on her feet were so tall, he couldn't believe she could stand upright in them.

Despite all that, what really grabbed his attention were the huge, white, feathery angel wings somehow attached to her back. They were as tall as Cree.

And good Lord, the woman was breathtaking.

Tristan knew he should say something, but he couldn't form the words.

Cree planted her hands on her hips and smirked. "What, nothing to say?"

"I'm... I'm trying, but I'm not sure I'm awake. Actually, I'm pretty sure I've died and gone to heaven, and the prettiest angel I've ever seen has greeted me at the pearly gates."

Cree stared at him for the longest and then burst out laughing. She laughed for a solid five minutes, tears filling her eyes, before she eventually composed herself.

"Man, you're good. Always knowing the perfect thing to say. I was planning to seduce you, but you just made it... weird," she said, chuckling.

With something in her hand, she pointed it toward the dresser and "All Night" by Beyonce poured through overhead speakers.

"Let's see if I can snap you out of whatever trance you've fallen under," she said as she started swaying her hips to the music, and Tristan's mouth went dry when she slowly began taking off her clothes.

A memory of her stripping for him early in their relationship came to mind, and his erection strained against his boxer briefs. He'd had mixed feelings when he learned she'd done a stint as a stripper to make money for law school. Despite understanding her reason, letting other men see her gorgeous body hadn't sat right with him.

On the other hand, Tristan had been twenty-one at the time. He had felt like the luckiest bastard to not only be dating an older woman, but one of the sexiest and most beautiful women in the world.

Now, as she danced in front of him, moving provocatively to the music and swaying her hypnotic hips, it was taking every bit of control not to reach for her. But if history was any indication, she didn't like it when he interrupted her dance routines.

Besides, who was he to stop all this perfection in front of him? Instead, Tristan sat all the way up and watched as she miraculously removed the wings without missing a beat. Next came the bra, and his dick pulsed painfully with need. He had never in his life wanted a woman as much as he wanted this one.

When the music changed to "Get Low" by Lil Jon & The East Side Boyz, Tristan almost lost his shit. The way her breasts bounced with each move, and her pebbled nipples teasing him mercilessly, he wasn't sure how much more he could take. As he started stroking himself, he marveled at how talented she was at stripping. The woman had skills, and her luscious hourglass figure was what wet dreams were full of.

"Damn, baby," he said, scooting to the edge of the bed, tempted to reach for her, but she must've sensed it. She danced away from him and didn't seem to care that she was killing him slowly.

When Cree had discarded some of her clothes, leaving her in nothing but her bejeweled thong, nylons, and heels, Tristan couldn't take any more. He was off the bed and had her in his arms before he realized he had moved.

"You are..." he started, but the words died on his lips when he roughly captured her mouth with his. His control was shot, and he kissed her long and hard.

Cree was right there with him, kissing him back as she ground against his painfully hard erection. A little bit more and his dick would be punching a hole right through his boxer briefs.

"I want you... now!" Cree rasped, her breaths coming in short spurts as she wrapped a leg around him.

Tristan didn't have to be told twice. He didn't bother stripping her of the rest of her sexy outfit. He unhooked her garter from the stockings, pulled his dick from his briefs, and then he moved her thong to the side. Unable to wait any longer, he thrust into her sweet heat and groaned with pleasure as her inner muscles gripped him like a tight fist.

Cree hissed, moaned, and rocked her hips in rhythm with his, pulling him in deeper each time he thrust into her. She gave herself over to him completely, but Tristan wanted to feel more of her. All of her.

"Hold on, baby," he ground out and her arms went around his neck as he gripped the back of her thighs, lifting her off the floor. With the wall offering additional support, he reentered her and pounded into her wetness like a man possessed.

Damn. He was on fire, and his hunger for her grew more intense as he devoured her mouth. He couldn't get enough, and he knew his release was near. And if the erotic moans and whimpers Cree was making as their bodies mated was any indication, her control was also slipping.

"Trist—oh, yes!" she cried out. "Yes, baby! Don't stop. Please don't stop," she chanted seconds before she jerked, screamed his name, and tightened around him, losing herself as they came together.

Tristan cursed under his breath as he struggled to pull air into his lungs. His release was powerful enough to take him out at the knees, but he hung on. Chests heaving, beads of sweat peppering his hairline, he managed to keep them both upright.

"That was intense," Cree said, slumping against him, and Tristan placed a lingering kiss on the side of her head.

"I love that you're built like a Mack truck and just as strong because I don't think I can stand on my own two legs," she said into the crook of his neck, and Tristan laughed.

Holding Cree up with one arm, he readjusted them and tucked himself back into his briefs before carrying her to the bed. She barely stirred while he stripped her out of the rest of her costume, tossing the items to the floor. His boxer briefs were quickly added to the pile.

By the time he climbed onto the bed, Cree was asleep, and Tristan chuckled. Some things never changed.

As he curled up next to her, his eyes grew heavier by the second, and his last thought before sleep consumed him was that he couldn't wait to do this all over again.

Chapter Twenty-One

The next morning, Tristan woke to the smell of coffee, but it was too early. Too early to open his eyes. Too early to move. It was even too early for coffee as far as he was concerned. Surely, he had just closed his eyes. There was no way it could be morning already. Not when he was still exhausted and felt as if he could sleep a week.

He lifted his wrist, surprised he had slept in his watch, and squinted at the face of the expensive time piece.

Five-thirty in the morning? Why the hell was Cree up so early? She didn't have to be to work until eight, or maybe it was nine. Whatever time she needed to be there didn't warrant her being up at the butt-crack of dawn.

Since retiring, Tristan rarely got up before nine, and even now, he had every intention of going back to sleep. But first, he needed to check on Cree.

As he thought about his gorgeous woman, a smile crept across his lips. The day before had been one for the books. It was official. Cree was finally his again, and this time it was for keeps. His *win-Cree-back* plan was working, but of course his

163

life wouldn't be complete until he had everything back that he had lost thirteen years ago. He wanted it all and more—his wife, a home, and kids someday. He wouldn't give up on that dream. Life was short and could end in a heartbeat.

Tristan had found that out when he got hurt. Yes, he lived to tell about it, though at the time, he felt as if he was dying. One minute he was a superstar on the football field, and the next minute, doctors were telling him he wouldn't be able to play again.

In his mind, his whole world had been ripped from him, and he hadn't known what to do. Football was his everything, and when it was over, he'd had to take a long look at his life and what he wanted to do with it going forward.

That's when he'd made the decision that he'd do whatever he could to get Cree back. Though he had tried years ago, this time failure hadn't been an option. She had always been in his heart, and now she was a part of all his future plans. His life had been incomplete without her in it.

If Tristan didn't learn anything else over the last few months, he learned you couldn't take anything for granted. Time didn't wait for anyone, and there were no guarantees that he and Cree would be alive tomorrow. So he wanted to take full advantage of every minute.

On that thought, he really should go in search of Cree and grab some coffee. But before he got up, the bedroom door slid open, and there she was wearing his shirt while holding two coffee mugs. Her hair was sticking up here and there and her face was scrubbed free of makeup. Yet, she was still the most beautiful woman to him.

His shirt stopped just below her gorgeous ass giving him an unobstructed view of everything below that. His gaze ran the length of her bare legs down to her hot pink toenails. "You have the prettiest legs I've ever seen," he said. Not only were they flawless and shapely, but they were nice and long, seeming to go on forever.

Then memories of her performance the night before flashed through his mind. That and her incredible costume which had showed off all her most impressive physical assets. Tristan would love a repeat of her striptease.

"Good morning, Mr. Irresistible, and thank you. I'm glad you like them," she said, her voice husky as if she'd just woken up. She lifted the mugs in her hand. "I took a chance on you wanting coffee. If not, you can pretend to drink it while I drink mine. So I don't have to drink alone."

He chuckled and leaned against the headboard while pulling the covers up to his waist. As Cree handed him one of the mugs, she bent down and gave him a lingering kiss on the lips. Yeah, this was how he wanted to wake up every day—with her wearing his shirt and her mouth anywhere on his body.

"Good morning, beautiful," he said when she pulled back. "Why are you up so early?"

Cree strolled to the other side of the bed and climbed in. "I usually wake up pretty early so I can ease into the day. Besides, we fell asleep before ten last night."

That was true. They'd fallen asleep earlier than he usually went to bed.

After taking a few careful sips of the steaming brew, Tristan sat his mug on the nightstand and then reached for Cree's cup to do the same.

"Come here," he said as he wrapped his arm around her shoulders and pulled her closer. When she was snug against his body, Tristan kissed her again, savoring her tantalizing lips. When he dipped his tongue into her mouth, she tasted like coffee and chocolate which might've been from the creamer she added to her mug.

As their tongues tangled, he pulled her even closer to

where she was draped across his chest and cradled in his arms. He dominated her mouth, savoring the moment, and seriously thinking about stripping her of his shirt.

His hand glided along the side of her leg, marveling in the softness of her skin. But when his hand inched below the shirt, her cell phone alarm went off.

"Maybe if we ignore it, it'll shut itself off," he murmured against her lips, and Cree laughed and pushed herself up.

"I don't know what type of fancy phone you have, but mine is not that sophisticated," she said as she turned off the alarm.

"Neither is mine. I don't think." He honestly didn't know and had never thought about that type of feature.

She scooted back against the headboard. "Can you hand me my mug?"

He did and grabbed his too. "What time do you have to be to work?" he asked as they enjoyed their coffee.

"I'm working from home today, and I'll probably start around nine."

"How often do you work remotely?" Asking that question made him realize just how much he still didn't know about her routines.

"Not often. Maybe once or twice a month. Since you stayed the night, I thought it would be nice to spend more time with you."

"I like the way you think. Though it's early as hell, I can think of a few things we can do before you clock in to work."

Cree chuckled. "I'm sure you can, but you're going to have to wait until I finish at least one cup of coffee."

"I really enjoyed hanging out with your family yesterday."

Shortly before they'd left, her sister Dorian and her fiancé, as well as Zion's wife and twins arrived. The cottage wasn't very big. They all were practically on top of each other. Still, he had a good time. Her father had mentioned that they needed to find a bigger place, but he was having a hard time convincing Mrs. Priestly. She thought it more convenient to live behind the B & B, and since they both worked there daily, Mr. Priestly hadn't pushed.

Tristan immediately thought that, if he and Cree got a place together, they could get one big enough to have both families over at the same time. He could already envision him having a man-cave for him and the guys to watch football on Sundays.

"I saw you with your niece and nephew yesterday," he said. "You're a natural with the babies, and it's clear they adore you."

"Aren't they the cutest?" Cree gushed. "They are the happiest, easy-going babies I've ever met. Rarely do they cry, and they'll let anyone hold them. But I'm curious to see if they're going to turn into little terrors when they start walking. That's how Zion was when he was little."

Tristan smiled at how animated Cree was as she told him more about the babies and how they reminded her of her brother when he was little. Though she didn't spend as much time with the twins as she'd like, it was clear she enjoyed them whenever they did get together. She explained how excited everyone was to have little ones around again because there hadn't been any babies since her nephew, Tray, was little, and now he was in college.

"You used to want children," Tristan said. "Is that still the case?"

Tristan felt her stiffen beside him, and he glanced at her. Her gaze was on the windows across the room, where the blinds were still closed, and she folded her lower lip between her teeth.

When she didn't respond, Tristan bumped her shoulder with his. "Cree? What's up?"

She stared down at the half-full mug in her hand and

breathed in deeply, then released the breath slowly. Unease clawed through Tristan. What was on her mind? Did she not want children anymore? And how would he feel if she said no? It wouldn't be a deal breaker, but he would definitely be disappointed. He wanted kids, and he wanted them with her.

"Yes, I'd love to have a couple of children," she finally said, her voice low and raspy before she cleared her throat.

Why did he feel a *but* coming? She still wouldn't look at him and that unease he had felt a few minutes ago was back but stronger.

"Talk to me," he said and set his coffee down, then removed her mug from her hands again and set it on the side table. He turned to better look at her. "What's wrong? Clearly something is bothering you. If you're wondering if I want kids, I do, but only if I have them with you."

"God, Tristan," she said, the words sounding as if they were ripped from her. "I hate when you say sweet things like that."

He could hear the tears in her voice, and now he was really concerned.

Wrapping his arm around her, he pulled her against him. "What is it? If you can't have children, that's okay, we'll figure something out. Just tell me what's wrong."

"I don't know how to tell you," she said barely above a whisper and then pulled out of his hold.

"Oh no you don't." He grabbed hold of her hand when she started to climb off the bed. "No more running, Cree. Remember, we're in this together. You and me. So whatever is going on, we'll deal with it together, but you need to talk to me. I can't fix it if I don't know what I'm dealing with."

"Even if you know, there's nothing you can do to fix it!" she snapped, her chest heaving as if she had just finished running a few blocks.

Still, Tristan didn't let go of her, but that unease from before was turning into fear.

Whatever was wrong was bad. Really bad if her watery eyes were any indication. Cree shedding tears twice in twenty-four hours wasn't good. Except for the day they'd gone their separate ways, he had never seen her cry until yesterday.

When she tugged her hand, trying to get out of his hold, this time Tristan let her go. She didn't go far. She sat on the edge of the bed quietly with her back to him.

One thing Tristan had learned early on when dealing with Cree was that she didn't share her feelings until she was ready to. While she sat there, he got up and slipped into his underwear. Grabbing his duffel bag from the chair, he went into the bathroom to shower.

He'd give her time to decide whether she planned to talk to him. While also bracing himself for whatever she might share. He just hoped that, whatever it was, they could get past it.

Chapter Twenty-Two

The moment Tristan disappeared into the bathroom, Cree released the breath she hadn't realized she'd been holding. She shouldn't have opened her big mouth. It wasn't necessary for her to share a secret she had planned to take to her grave, but there was a part of her that couldn't lie to Tristan. Not even by omission.

She stood. With the conversation they needed to have, she needed to be wearing more than just a shirt. She pulled lounging pajamas from the top drawer of her dresser and hurried into them. What the hell was she going to say to Tristan? Her plan had been to leave the past in the past. Yet, somehow it kept popping up at every turn.

After sliding on a pair of thick socks, she took her coffee and left the room. It was a little early for breakfast, but cooking helped her relax.

"Omelets could work."

As she pulled ingredients from the refrigerator, Tristan strolled into the kitchen. He must not have seen his T-shirt that she had left on the bed because all he had on was a pair of pants and socks. The upper half of his body—his strong, muscular, no-fat-nowhere body, was bare. All that deliciousness on full display for her eyes only, and boy, did she want to...

"Cree!"

She startled, and her eyes leaped up to meet his. "What?"

"I called your name like ten times. I asked if you want some help, but clearly, I must be distracting you. What? You can't focus with all this in your presence?" he asked, flexing his biceps and making his pecks dance.

Good Lord, the man was too fine and sexy for his own good, and right now it was pissing her off. She couldn't lure him out of the kitchen and back to the bedroom for some wild and sweaty sex since they needed to talk.

"You're right, I can't," she said seriously, emotionally preparing herself for a conversation she didn't want to have.

Tristan searched her eyes for a second before he nodded and went back upstairs. While he did that, she started chopping vegetables for their omelets.

I can do this, she told herself. *It's the right thing to do.*

A few minutes later, she glanced up when Tristan returned, wearing a shirt she hadn't seen before, and she remembered he had brought clothes with him. Returning her attention back to the cutting board, she continued chopping vegetables.

"Walking away from you was the hardest thing I've ever done," she started and grabbed a green pepper to cut up. She slashed it in half, probably with more force than needed, and Tristan moved to her side. He put his hand over hers and slowly removed the knife from her grasp, setting it on the counter next to the stove.

Cree let him. It probably wasn't a good idea to be swinging a knife right now.

She had just huffed out a breath when Tristan stood behind

her. He wrapped his strong arms around her, and Cree melted against his hard body.

"I hope you know you can talk to me about anything," he said and placed a kiss on the side of her head. "I'm not going anywhere."

Cree's body trembled involuntarily. Not because she was cold, but because she wasn't. There wasn't much that made her uncomfortable, but the last twenty-four hours had brought its share of uncomfortable moments. Which was probably good. She had buried the past instead of taking time to deal with it.

Tristan tightened his hold, and Cree wasn't sure if his nearness was helping or making it harder to speak. Emotions swirled inside of her like butterflies taking flight in her gut, making her feel as if she were going to puke. Seconds ticked by as they stood in her kitchen next to the center island while she tried to figure out where to start.

She inhaled deeply and then released the breath before saying, "When I walked away from you, I didn't know I was pregnant."

After a slight hesitation, as if he needed to process her words, Tristan stiffened. Cree wasn't sure, but it also seemed like he stopped breathing for a minute. Without a word, his arms fell away from her and he stumbled backwards, and she missed his warmth immediately.

"Cree," he said, and that one simple word held so much anguish, disbelief, and a hint of pleading in his tone.

He went to the opposite side of the counter, adding more distance between them, and faced her. Shock and fear marred his handsome face.

"Please tell me you didn't have an..." His words trailed off, and she swallowed hard.

"I didn't."

She bit down on her lower lip as stupid tears filled her eyes, but there was no way in hell she would let them fall. She had cried for what seemed like months after she and Tristan broke up. She shouldn't have any tears left. Yet, emotion clogged her throat, and a rogue tear slipped down her cheek before she quickly wiped it away.

"At twelve weeks, I had a miscarriage." Her voice cracked on the last word, and she cleared her throat.

Her chest heaved and her heart cracked as she struggled to keep her emotions in check, but she was failing miserably. Everything inside of her wanted to cry out and throw something for the heartbreaking pain she had endured thirteen years ago.

Instead, she braced her hands on the counter and stared down at the gleaming hardwood floor. She couldn't look at Tristan, but she could tell he hadn't moved from his spot on the other side of the counter. He stood there motionless, and Cree couldn't even imagine what he was thinking.

There'd been days when that time in her life seemed like a bad dream. A dream that invaded her peace of mind at the same time every year. The death date of her baby... their baby.

"You didn't tell me," Tristan said barely above a whisper. "How could you not tell me? You went through that, and you never said a word. Were you ever going to tell me?"

Cree didn't respond. She couldn't. Still choked up, she couldn't say anything and risk bursting into tears.

"Of course you weren't," he continued with a humorless laugh. "Dammit, Cree! You should've told me we were having a baby!" he roared and pounded on the counter. "I deserved to know that I was going to be a father. No matter how things turned out, I should've known!"

The hurt in his words was her undoing as a few more tears slipped through, but she batted them away. He was right, he had deserved to know, but it didn't matter because the baby hadn't survived.

She finally looked up and met his angry, teary eyes. "I wanted our baby more than I have ever wanted anything in my life," she ground out, anger and hurt warring inside of her. "I had already lost you, and losing our child nearly killed me."

That was an understatement. With all that had been going on in her life at the time, she had fallen into a deep depression that she thought she'd never get from under. It had seemed her whole world was crumbling around her, and if it hadn't been for Essence, she wasn't sure where she'd be right now. Her sister had been her rock, listening to her, wiping her tears, and making sure she didn't totally lose herself to grief. Cree owed her so much.

Cree wiped her eyes and cheeks with the heel of her hand. "I always knew I'd want kids one day. When I found out I was pregnant, it gave me hope that my life wasn't completely a mess. I didn't find out I was pregnant until I was eight weeks, and I'd been shocked. I had also been in denial since we were careful with birth control, but there'd been so much going on. Days were running into each other. They were a blur, and I lost track of many of them.

"But Tristan, I did plan on telling you about the baby. I just hadn't decided on when or how. You were heading to Philly, and I was... Well, I'd been trying to come to grips with... everything, especially keeping my business afloat." She shook her head. Those years seemed like a lifetime ago, while also feeling as if she had experienced everything yesterday. "After I lost the baby..."

"God, Cree," Tristan started, but stopped and ran his large hands down his face.

He had decreased the distance between them, but he was still out of reach, which was probably good. If he came any closer or touched her, she'd probably fall apart. As it was, she was barely hanging on.

"I couldn't tell you afterwards because I blamed you for everything. I know it wasn't fair, but I blamed you for betraying me by signing with Ralph. I blamed you for putting my sports agency at risk, and I blamed you for every stress in my life. Which I figured caused the miscarriage. For the longest time, I blamed *you* for me losing our child."

Tristan made a sound that was a cross between a sob and a growl, and he turned his back to her. With his hands resting on top of his head, he moved away from the counter and went to the opening of the kitchen before stopping abruptly.

With his back to her, he said, "I am so sorry, Cree. I never meant to hurt you," he choked out. "God knows I never meant for *any* of this to happen. You were my everything!"

Cree's heart cracked at his emotion-filled words, and she started to tell him that she was just as much at fault, but he continued.

"I honestly thought by signing with Ralph that I was doing what was best for us... for the family I wanted to build with you. With the large contracts he was known for getting his clients, I knew if he could do the same for us, we'd be set for life. I never thought—"

"You never thought I'd react before thinking. You never thought I would toss you out of the apartment before giving you a chance to explain your reasoning," Cree finished for him, though that probably wasn't what he was going to say. Tristan didn't blame her for their breakup. He never blamed her, but deep down, she had always known she'd been the one at fault. Sure, he shouldn't have made such an important decision without talking to her first, but ultimately, she was the one who had ended their relationship.

"I'll never be able to forgive myself for destroying what we had," he said as if not hearing what she'd said, and then he rushed toward the stairs.

"Tristan, wait!"

Cree went after him, but he had already made it to the top of the landing and didn't look back.

She cursed under her breath. "What have I done?"

Chapter Twenty-Three

Tristan stumbled into Cree's bedroom, unsure of how he made it up the stairs in one piece. His body was moving on its own accord as he walked around in circles in her space, aimlessly looking for something but really not seeing anything.

A baby.

Cree had been pregnant.

He'd been a dad.

Miscarriage.

As the words flowed through his brain on a loop, Tristan sank deeper into some type of emotional dark abyss, struggling to pull himself together. His head swam. His hands shook. His heart pounded like a jackhammer.

He rubbed his chest as if that would help settle the unsteadiness he was feeling. "Shoes. I need my shoes," he mumbled, looking around the room until he found them sticking from under the bed.

He grabbed them, then started to sit on the edge of the bed

but missed and almost landed on the floor until he caught himself.

Okay. Just breathe. In for four. Out for four.

He did that a few times until he felt he had regained some of his control.

Slowly sitting on the bed, he remained still for a few seconds before he bent forward and started slipping on his shoes. Before he could tie them up, he heard Cree at the door and froze. He couldn't look at her. He'd been serious when he said he'd never forgive himself for hurting her.

A baby.

They had created a baby together, and because of him, she had lost their child.

He propped his elbows on his thighs and put his face in his hands. Saying he was sorry wasn't enough to fix this. Giving her office space and finding her clients for her agency couldn't fix this. Nothing could fix what he had done to her, what he had done to them.

Tristan startled when Cree placed her hand on his back, and he lurched off the bed, stumbling away from her.

"I'll be out of here in a minute," he said, and grabbed his duffel. He didn't bother tying his shoestrings. He just needed to leave her alone once and for all.

"Tristan please," Cree said when he was almost at the bedroom door. "Don't leave. You told me no more running, and now I'm saying the same to you. No running."

He braced a hand on the doorframe to help hold him up, and his shoulders sagged. He felt hollow inside. Like someone had ripped out his heart and stomped it to death. He didn't know what to do in this situation. He was so out of his element, running felt like the only solution.

"Please don't leave me," she said, gutting him even more.

"Cree, you deserve better. I knew it years ago, and now..."

"And now you're crazy if you think there's a better man out there than you. And even if there was, and there isn't, you're the only one I want. You're mine, and I will fight like hell to keep you," she bit out.

Her voice was closer, and when he turned around, she was within arm's reach of him.

He needed to say something, but looking at her beautiful face and watery eyes, the words wouldn't come. Emotions clogged his throat, and he was all choked up.

Without a word, Cree stepped toward him and placed her hand on his chest. "I don't want you to leave, and you know I always get what I want." There was humor in her tone, but Tristan couldn't laugh. He couldn't smile. He could barely look at her without wanting to fall to his knees and beg her forgiveness over and over again.

She opened her arms to him, and it was his undoing. He dropped his bag to the floor and crushed her to him. Burying his face into the crook of her scented neck, it was taking all he had not to cry like a damn baby. Instead, he closed his eyes and breathed her in.

Cree whispered words of comfort in his ear, telling him he wasn't the one at fault. Reminding him that they'd been young and dumb, both making mistakes in the relationship. She apologized for ever blaming him for their failed relationship, promising to listen before reacting in the future.

"I love you," she whispered. "I love you so much, and I don't want you to leave. *Ever.* Promise me you won't leave me, even if I'm stupid enough to try to push you away. Promise you won't leave."

"I won't," he said, his voice thick with emotion. "I'm never leaving you. I love you too much, and I need you in my life, Cree."

As he held her in his arms, Tristan didn't think he could

ever let her go. Yeah, he thought he could walk out the door and leave her alone, thought that would be the best for both of them. He was wrong and was lying to himself. He might've messed up back then, but he planned to spend the rest of his life showing her how much he loved her.

Tristan wasn't sure how long they stood that way, but the longer he held her in his arms, some of the anxiousness fell away. They were going to make it. They had to. He couldn't envision his future without her in it.

After another few minutes of holding her close, he placed a kiss close to her ear, then lifted his head. He cupped her face between his hands, and with the pad of his thumb, he brushed a couple of errant tears from her cheeks.

"I can't apologize enough for my role in everything that happened to us, but please forgive me, baby."

It wasn't until she wiped his face that he realized a few tears had slipped through.

"I already have, Tristan. I forgive both of us. What happened back in the day, despite what I once thought, wasn't on you. I accept responsibility for my role in that mess. We can't go back and fix what happened, but we can move forward and try to get it right this time. So, you can't just leave." She shrugged. "You're mine. You belong to me."

Tristan chuckled though his heart still ached. Still cupping her face, he bent down and kissed her.

"I love you so damn much. Thank you for giving us another chance. I won't let you down."

"Me too," she said and covered his mouth with hers. The kiss started slow and tender, but soon they were both moaning.

Tristan slid his hands down her body, then gripped her butt cheeks before lifting her. Cree's legs immediately went around his waist, and he slowly carried her across the room.

"I had my heart set on making omelets for us, but I think we need to kiss and make up properly before we eat," she said as he neared the bed.

Tristan nodded as she peppered kisses on his face.

"Yeah, you're probably right. Did I mention I love you?" he asked as he laid her on the bed, but she kept her arms around his neck and grinned.

"You might've mentioned it a time or two. Now I'm expecting you to show me."

A smile played on Tristan's mouth, and he brought his lips inches from hers. "I think I can handle that."

Chapter Twenty-Four

It had been a month since the baby conversation, and Cree could honestly say it had brought her and Tristan closer. Granted, the days that followed their talk had still been a little tense since Tristan blamed himself. Yet, Cree kept reiterating that he hadn't been to blame, and in order for them to have a future, they had to stop dwelling on the past.

It took awhile, but he had finally come around and lately had been talking more about their future. A future she wanted with him. Which was something she once thought she'd never have again but thank goodness for second chances. Having Tristan back in her life made her realize she hadn't been doing much living. Working from sunup to sundown with the occasional family event tossed in wasn't living.

No, living might include those things, but it also included looking forward to going home to the man you loved. It included enjoying the simple things in life like showering together, going on evening walks after a rough day at work, and even sitting at the kitchen counter, snacking on grapes, while watching her man cook for her.

Cree found herself grinning throughout the day at something he did or said, and these days, she looked forward to any time they got to spend together. She could admit to being happier than she'd been in a long time.

They were currently in Atlanta where Tristan had been working on an endorsement project, and the production company had given him the royal treatment. She and Tristan were in a hotel suite that could rival any luxury apartment, and from the moment Cree walked into it two days ago, she had felt at home.

She'd stayed in her share of beautiful hotels, but nothing like this one. The suite included top of the line everything from chandeliers to soaking tubs, and it even had a baby grand piano in the corner of the living room. The service from the hotel staff was also top-notch.

She wasn't looking forward to leaving the two-bedroom, two-and-a-half-bathroom suite that looked like something out of *Luxury Travel* magazine. But at least now she knew how the other half lived.

"Damn, I've missed you," Tristan said as he sipped his champagne while rubbing her legs that were in his lap.

"Not as much as I've missed you." She tried to lower her legs so she could lean over and kiss him, but Tristan held firm.

They had just finished eating dinner—sushi, shrimp tempura, and a cucumber salad—and were still sitting at the round, dining table. After his photo shoot earlier, they had returned to the hotel so that they could make up for the time they'd been apart. The week and a half with him in Atlanta and her in Chicago had felt more like months, and she wasn't looking forward to doing it again any time soon.

She had wanted to arrive the week before but work obligations had kept her away. Everything worked out well, though, because this weekend was family weekend at Clark Atlanta

University where her nephew attended. Not only was she spending some much-needed time with Tristan, but she'd also get to hang out with her nephew, Tray, as well as Essence and Jackson.

"You look good in my shirt," Tristan said, as his large hand crept higher on her leg, and she tried not to moan. His sensual touch, even on her legs, felt like an erotic caress that stirred her desire for him. After a couple of rounds of sex this evening, she should've had her fill, but nope, she wanted him again.

As for the shirt, she had slipped into the light-blue dress shirt, which he had discarded earlier when room service showed up sooner than she thought they would.

"And you look good in nothing but your sweatpants," she said, and he grinned.

His sculpted upper body was on full display, showing off his brawny chest, sinewy muscles, and rippling abs. The man's body from head to toe was like a piece of art. As far as Cree was concerned, he never had to wear shirts—or clothes for that matter—around the house. She'd love nothing more than to admire his mouth-watering physique 24/7.

When her gaze met his eyes, she smiled at the way he was staring at her, like she hung the moon and the stars. The love she saw in his eyes made her feel all tingly inside. She didn't think she could miss anyone as much as she had missed him while she was stuck in Chicago.

Still holding on to her legs with one hand, Tristan ate another piece of sushi. "My real estate agent called," he said. "She found a house in Wilmette for me to look at when I return to Chicago."

Cree frowned. "I thought you were trying to find some-place near the lake, not the suburbs."

"I was, but when you and I were talking about houses a

couple of weeks ago, you mentioned you like Wilmette and the Hinsdale area. So, I told her to adjust her search."

Cree didn't know what to say. Seemed she fell in love with this man more each day. He'd always been a good listener, but she hadn't expected him to change his house hunt because of her. Honestly, the way her heart beat for him these days, she didn't care what part of town they lived in. She'd follow him to the end of the earth.

"Tristan, I—"

"I want you to move in with me. Which means I need to find a place that you would like to live in. Actually, I think it's time for you to join this house hunt."

He'd been looking at more places lately, especially now that he had accepted an offer on his family's huge home, and his parents had found a house. He had told Cree that, now that everyone else was situated, he could focus more on his future, which included her.

Cree lowered her legs and moved her chair closer to his. "I want us to move in together, but don't change your search criteria for me. If you want to live in a condo overlooking the lake, I can handle that."

She placed a tender kiss on his lips before releasing him.

"I can live anywhere as long as you're there with me. So, we'll find a house in the suburbs."

Her heart squeezed, and she smiled as she straddled his lap. Wrapping her arms around his neck, she said, "I've been thinking."

She placed a whisper of a kiss on his lips as she stared into his loving eyes. This man made her so happy that there were times, like now, when she felt as if she'd burst. Agreeing to a second chance with him was the best decision she ever made.

Tristan squeezed her bare thighs, effectively pulling her out of her thoughts. "What have you been thinking about?"

"*You.* I thought about what you said about not wanting to travel for endorsements, and I get why. I've missed you so much, I almost broke down last week and hopped a flight here despite some important meetings."

"God, I would've loved that." He gently brushed her long bangs away from her eyes, something he did often, and her heart fluttered. "I missed you so damn much, I've decided even three days apart is too many. We need to revisit those other endorsement deals. Oh, and I'm not interested in any coaching positions unless they're in Chicago or you're planning to travel with me."

"Umm, don't say no to those yet. The offers, as they stand right now, are incredible, and we haven't even started negotiations yet. But we'll talk about those when we return to Chicago. There's something else I want to discuss," she said, her heart rate inching up as she reached into the pocket of the shirt she was wearing. "I love you even more than I did the first time we married. I know you said you're in this for the long haul, and so am I." She held up the platinum wedding band that she had purchased recently. "I was wondering... will you marry me again?"

Tristan's mouth dropped open when his gaze landed on the ring, and several emotions flashed across his features—shock, admiration, but then his eyebrows pulled together into a frown.

"Dammit, Cree! Why are you—"

"Your ass better not say no." She slapped his hard chest playfully. Considering how many times he had brought up marriage in conversations, she knew he was on the same page as her. She just wasn't sure why his handsome face was scowling.

"I won't say no if you don't say no," he said and pulled a Tiffany blue box from somewhere under the table.

Now Cree was the one sitting with her mouth hanging open.

"Tonight, I had planned for us to have a nice romantic dinner at a ridiculously expensive restaurant where we could eat steak and seafood. Not this bird food you ordered from room service. But no, you insisted on us having a quiet night in, and you had a taste for sushi. Now, you're messing up my proposal with one of your own. What the hell, babe?"

Cree covered her mouth and laughed. She laughed even harder when she reached for the jewelry box and he pulled it out of reach. "Don't blame me for getting the jump on you, and besides, you could've said no."

Tristan chuckled and shook his head. "What am I going to do with you? You're the most stubborn, infuriating, and play-too-much, woman I know. Don't think I haven't noticed you grinding your bare ass on top of me while I'm trying to have a serious moment here."

Cree couldn't help it. She laughed again, and she definitely knew he noticed because his erection, though behind his pants, was hard between her legs.

"With all that said," he continued and turned serious, "I don't want to live a life without you. When I lost you and our marriage ended, I thought I'd never find happiness again. Then fast forward thirteen years, and putting up with your stubbornness, that joy I thought I lost returned when you came back into my life.

"You're that missing piece I need to make my life complete, and I don't want to go another day without you knowing just how much I love and adore you. I want to build a life with you. I want to wake up every day with you snuggled against me in my arms. And I also..." He swallowed hard and glanced away before returning his gaze to her. "I also want to have children with you. As many as you'll give me."

He opened the lid of the box, and Cree gasped. Her hand flew to her chest as she gawked at the gorgeous emerald-cut diamond ring that had to be at least five carats, the stone clear and blinding.

"Will you marry me? And you better not say no."

They both laughed, and she wrapped her arms around his neck and held on tightly. "I want everything you want, and I'd love to marry you," she said close to his ear, before pulling back.

Tristan slipped the ring onto her finger, and then his lips covered hers. Their tantalizing kiss sang through her veins, and Cree's senses reeled. If someone would have told her even a year ago that the man she never stopped loving would come back into her life and ask her to marry him, she would've called them crazy. Thrilled they were getting their second chance, she couldn't wait to be his wife.

Unable to help herself, she ground on top of him. The friction from his sweatpants against her mound already had her wet for him, and she moaned against his mouth. Even through his clothing, she could feel how hard he was, but she wanted to feel him inside of her.

Before she could demand he take off his pants, he lifted slightly with her still on top of him and slid them down before reclaiming his seat. Cree started to readjust herself so she could slide down on top of him, but he gripped her waist hard enough to hold her still.

"Just so we're clear," he said through gritted teeth as if he was barely hanging on and already on the verge of losing control, "no more going to the door to let in room service when you're not wearing any panties. That shirt is thick, but it ain't that damn thick. I don't want anybody else seeing what's mine."

Cree snorted and gripped his shoulders as she lifted up. "Are we doing this or are you going to keep barking out orders?" she asked as she slowly lowered herself onto his thick shaft.

He was in the middle of saying something else but hissed when she settled on top of him, and her inner walls hugged him tightly. She felt all of him, his long, thick shaft filling her completely.

A dizzying pleasure swirled inside of her while Tristan gripped her hips, with all his unbelievable strength, and slid her up and down his length. The man was hella strong, and with each thrust, some of her control seeped away.

"Oh, baby, *yessss,*" she purred as they moved together.

Tristan's hands moved from her hips to the buttons on his shirt. After his fingers fumbled with one of them, he let out a string of curses before ripping the shirt open, buttons flying everywhere.

Cree started to laugh, but it turned into a whimper when he palmed her breasts. He pushed them together, squeezing and kneading them as he sucked on one of her nipples and then the other.

Lust-filled pressure built inside of her as she rotated her hips on top of him and with each lap of his tongue.

Tristan mumbled against her skin, but she couldn't make out what he was saying. Yet, she had a pretty good idea when he tore his mouth from her breasts and gripped her hips. He was close to his release as he drove into her while also lifting her up and down, slamming her onto his erection.

She was close too, and she started to tell him when her words were cut off by an orgasm that stole her breath.

A harsh moan filled the quietness in the room, and Cree wasn't sure if it was his or hers. All she knew was that she would never get enough of him.

Collapsing against each other, they held each other tightly as aftershocks shook them both. It took minutes for their breathing to get back to normal, and when it did, Cree released a contented sigh. That was so good.

Tristan was still buried inside of her when his stomach growled, and Cree chuckled.

"See what your sushi does to me?" he grumbled, and Cree lifted her head to look at him. "It leaves me so damn hungry that even the best sex is not enough to distract my stomach."

Cree laughed at the way his brows dipped into a frown in mock disgust.

"I'm ordering a steak and some potatoes from the restaurant down the street. Do you want anything?"

She was still laughing when she cupped his cheeks and placed a breathy kiss on his lips. She felt so blessed to have this man in her life. "Nah, baby. I have everything I want right here."

Chapter Twenty-Five

Two days later, Cree was sitting in her nephew's dorm room, looking through an entertainment magazine while waiting for him to return. It was the first day of the university's family weekend, and she, Tristan, Essence and Jackson had started the day with a tour of the campus.

As Cree roamed around taking in the buildings, the various programs offered, and the students, all she kept thinking was that Tray was actually in college. Seemed like yesterday he was just a baby, and now he was an adult, majoring in mass media and preparing for his future.

After their tour, the five of them participated in various activities around campus and had a blast. It was also good to see her sister having a good time. Essence was missing Tray like crazy and had been fawning over him since arriving. Watching her laughing and loosening up some was good to see, and it helped Tray not feel as guilty about going away for school.

Now everyone had split up and gone their separate ways. Tristan, at the request of the athletic director, was hanging out with athletes at the school's sports facility. Jackson had talked

Essence into going with him to visit some friends in town, and that left Cree to hang out with Tray. He'd wanted to talk to her about something, and she was curious to find out what was on his mind. Only he had left her a few minutes ago because he needed to pick up a book from a friend.

As Cree sat at his desk waiting, she couldn't help but think about the argument she and Tristan had had earlier in the day. She had begged Tristan to understand it wasn't that she didn't want anyone to know about them. She just wanted to make sure that, with their announcement, the timing was right.

Though she wanted more than anything to share the news about their engagement, she didn't think it was a good idea. At least not yet. Tristan, as well as his retirement news, was still a hot topic in the sports world. The media wanted to know what he's been up to, his future plans, and any additional information they could get on him.

If she and Tristan happened to be photographed holding hands or stealing kisses, tongues would wag and speculations would soar. They had to be strategic about revealing their relationship. Which was why they'd been keeping their distance from each other while on campus, and they both hated it.

Still, she realized shortly after arriving on campus that not behaving like a couple right now was a good idea. The moment Tristan stepped on campus, faculty, students, and a few parents recognized him. Pictures were taken of him, autographs were signed, and an informal interview had taken place. Cree stayed in the background, but people wanted to know what he was doing there. He kept his responses vague, claiming he just happened to show up to see the campus during family weekend.

Despite their decision to not look as if they were together on campus, though, Tristan was wearing the wedding band she'd given him. If anyone had asked about it, she didn't know, but the gesture made her heart sing. Wearing the ring showed her how excited he was for them to be back together again.

In hindsight, she should've worn the one he had given her. She could've worn it on her right hand temporarily, and that still would've been better than her leaving it in the hotel's safe.

Cree shook her head in disgust. She had to do better. No way was she going to risk losing her man or causing any doubt in his mind of her love for him. She was excited about their reunion and couldn't wait for them to take the next step into their future.

"I'm going to make it up to him," she mumbled as an idea sparked in her mind. She was going to do whatever it took to show him that she was all in.

In the meantime, Cree had decisions to make regarding their professional relationship. Now that they were engaged, she might have to hand his account off to one of the firm's associates or a partner. That way there'd be no questions brought up about her, at some point, dating a client. Her relationship with her coworkers and her clients was important to her. She never wanted to do anything that would question her integrity or professionalism.

Tristan insisted he only wanted her to oversee his account. Which Cree would also prefer. She could do it without any questions if she moved forward with branching out on her own.

Decisions. Decisions.

"Sorry, Aunt Cree. I didn't think it would take me that long," Tray said as he hurried into the room, closing the door behind him.

Her nephew was almost six feet tall and as thin as a rail. Considering how much the kid ate, she had no idea how he managed to stay so skinny. Though he shared similar features of the Priestly family, with his sepia skin tone and full lips, he looked a lot like his biological father who Cree hadn't seen since high school.

"Tristan didn't come back yet?" Tray asked. "I still can't believe you know him. Mom said he might be your boyfriend, but you guys are keeping it quiet."

Cree laughed at his attempt at whispering. "Can you keep a secret?" she asked, knowing he could.

He nodded enthusiastically, his eyes wide in anticipation.

"Tristan is my fiancé, but we're not telling anyone yet," she said quietly.

"Wait. I'm the only one who knows?" he whisper-shouted.

"Yup, so if anyone finds out before we announce it, I'll know who leaked the news."

A huge grin spread across his face. "I won't say a word, but it is going to be so cool to finally tell people that Tristan Whitmore is my uncle. That's crazy! He might be able to get me tickets to see the Eagles or the Packers," he said of two of his favorite NFL teams.

Cree laughed at his excitement, and he was probably right. If asked, Tristan would definitely work his magic to hook Tray up with tickets to a game, especially the Eagles. As for the Packers, she knew for a fact that it wouldn't be easy to get tickets for a game played at Lambeau Field. Still, if anyone could get some, it would be Tristan.

"Did Dominic show up yet?"

"Nope, I haven't seen him," she said of his roommate.

"I hope you're still here when he does. His stepmom used to be a stuntwoman. How cool is that?"

"Very cool," she said and listened as he told her about his roommate and family.

"Aunt Cree, you have to talk to Mom because she's not

listening to me and Dad," Tray said quietly, and Cree straightened at the mention of his dad. "She's—"

"Wait. You've been in contact with your father?" she asked.

Essence hadn't mentioned her ex in years. As far as Cree knew, she hadn't talked to the loser since high school. She had gotten pregnant with Tray toward the end of her senior year, and her ex, Kyle, hadn't wanted anything to do with Tray.

Before Kyle learned he was going to be a father, he had received a basketball scholarship from Marquette University. He was good enough to go pro and wasn't letting anything or anyone stand in his way. Though he hadn't asked Essence to have an abortion, he had asked her to give the baby up for adoption.

Not surprisingly, Essence told him adoption wasn't an option, and she'd raise their child on her own. After Tray was born, Kyle had signed his rights away, and Cree assumed that was the end of it.

"You've met your father?"

"Yeah, I met him once, but we don't have a relationship. I'm not talking about him. I'm talking about Jackson."

"When did you start calling him *Dad*?"

Jackson and Essence had been friends for as long as Cree could remember, and he'd always been active in Tray's life. Cree just wished her sister could see what they all saw—that Jackson was crazy in love with her and Tray. He treated them like they belonged to him, and there was nothing he wouldn't do for either of them.

"This summer, a little bit before I moved to Atlanta, I started calling him *Dad*. He's more of a father than that sperm donor who—" As if catching himself from saying too much, he backpedaled. "I mean Kyle. My biological dad will never be my father. That would be Jackson, and before you ask, he's cool with it, and I'm thinking about changing my last name to his, even if Mom doesn't marry him."

Cree just stared at her nephew. He had grown up so fast. She still remembered when Essence brought him home from the hospital. She and her sister used to share a bedroom, and their parents had put a baby bed in there for Tray.

It seemed like a lifetime ago, and now here she was visiting her nephew in college. He had grown up to be thoughtful, funny, and an intelligent young man, who she was so proud of. Which was what she told him.

"But anyway," he said, interrupting her thoughts, "I wanted to talk to you because I need you to talk to Mom. She's threatening to move to Atlanta, and I don't want her to. I'm not a little kid where I need my mommy all the time, but she's not listening to me and Dad. I know she'll listen to you."

Cree held back a groan. She didn't have the heart to tell him that she had already tried talking his mother out of moving to Atlanta. Essence was seriously considering it, but maybe Cree could give it one more shot.

The dorm room door flew open.

"Come on, Dee. Why do I have to attend? Uncle Laz won't mind if I skip the awards banquet," Tray's roommate, Dominic, said as he and who Cree assumed were his parents filled the doorway.

Tray had already told her about them and how Dominic's stepmother, Dakota, used to be a stuntwoman. Tray had even shown her videos of the woman doing stunts on motorcycles, leaping from one rooftop to another, and he'd even found a YouTube video of her in a fight. Not only did the woman have a black belt in some martial art, but she also owned a dojo there in Atlanta.

As Cree watched them enter, her first thought was—what a beautiful couple. The man, tall and extremely good-looking had an authoritative presence, like he might've been former military or law enforcement. And she never would've guessed the woman was a daredevil. She was a little shorter than Cree and looked... normal. Like just another woman. Albeit a gorgeous supermodel-like woman, but still, just a woman.

"Oh, sorry. I didn't know anyone was here," Dominic said.

"That's okay. We were just hanging out," Tray said. "This is my Aunt Cree. She's the one who knows Tristan Whitmore, and he's on campus."

Dominic's eyes lit up. "For real? Do you think I could get his autograph?"

Dominic's father shook his head. "Forgive my son's manners. I'm Hamilton Crosby, and this is my wife, Dakota. It's nice to meet you."

"Oh, yeah, Aunt Cree. Ms. Dakota is the stuntwoman I was telling you about. Cool, right?"

All the adults laughed.

"Very cool," Cree said as they greeted each other.

Conversation flowed easily, and Cree learned that Dominic's father was part owner of Supreme Security—Atlanta. Which was the same agency her brother Zion worked for, except he was located in Chicago. Her brother often talked about *Atlanta's Finest,* which was the nickname given to the security specialists at the agency in Atlanta. Like the one in Chicago, the group was made up of former military and law enforcement personnel.

A knock sounded on the open door, and everyone glanced that way. The moment Cree saw Tristan standing there, butterflies took flight in her stomach and she swooned. The man was gorgeous, and he was hers.

"Whoa! Tristan Whitmore!" Dominic said and he and Tray rushed to the door, talking a mile a minute, and Cree laughed.

Tristan didn't miss a beat. He jumped right into conversation with the boys, as well as Dominic's parents, and her heart swelled. Even with a celebrity status, she loved how approachable Tristan was, and she fell more in love with him every day.

So why was she still willing to keep their relationship a secret?

It's time to quit hiding. Time to go public with their relationship. She'd figured out everything else later, but for now, she was determined to show her man how in love she was with him.

Once the conversation settled some, Cree walked toward him. He glanced over everyone's head and looked at her, giving her a sexy smile as she got closer. But his eyes searched hers as if wondering what she was up to.

He could read her so good. She did have a little something on her mind.

"Hey, baby," she said and kissed him sweetly, not caring who was watching. "I hope you're ready to go because I came up with some other plans for us while we're in town."

Cree had no doubt he was going to enjoy what she was cooking up.

Chapter Twenty-Six

With a glass of bourbon in his hand, Tristan leaned his back against the bar and stared out at the crowd. They were at Moody Days Jazz Club which Nyla, Cree's sister, owned, celebrating Cree's birthday. She had rented out the place for the night, and though Tristan had expected a small gathering, there were a hundred and twenty-five people in attendance.

Tristan rarely went out to clubs or parties, but he could honestly say he was having a good time. The party was jumping. There was plenty of food, drinks and a popular DJ, who'd been flown in from New York. Cree and her sisters had done a great job party planning and decorating the place. The black, white, and silver color scheme was sophisticated and elegant, and all the guests were dressed in at least one of those same colors.

He smiled as he spotted Cree moving fluidly on the dance floor. She was a natural, even with line dancing as she personalized some of the steps while staying in sync with everyone around her. How she moved with such grace in those super high heels was a mystery, but what really made her stand out was her outfit. She looked like a goddess in the daring, off-white jumpsuit that showed way more skin than Tristan preferred. The front of the garment crisscrossed over her breasts, leaving part of her torso and stomach bare, and her back was exposed.

The outfit was *hot*, and so was she.

"You haven't taken your eyes off her since I got here," Bethany, who was wearing all black, said over the music as she approached him, carrying a glass of wine.

"She makes it hard to look away," he said of Cree and wrapped his arm around Bethany's shoulders, drawing her close. "Having a good time?"

"I am. It's a nice party, and Cree's siblings are cool."

"They are, and I'm glad you and Quincy were able to make it."

"Yeah, me too."

The day after he and Cree returned from Atlanta, he and Bethany had met for lunch at her request. Tristan couldn't remember the last time he had spent time with his sister without arguing about something. Yet that day, they'd had a good conversation. She had apologized to him for her behavior over the last few months, promising she wasn't as bratty as she'd been acting.

Like him, she was pivoting, trying to figure out her next steps and what else she wanted to do with her life. He understood the headache that came with that, especially when you weren't quite sure what you wanted to do.

During that conversation, he had also found out she had moved out of the condo in Philly. She had also found her own place in Chicago that she was moving into shortly before Thanksgiving. Which was good timing since his parents had found a new home, and Tristan had accepted an offer on the family house.

But what really shocked Tristan was when Bethany had asked to officially meet Cree so she could apologize to her. The three of them had dinner together, which went well, and Cree had invited her and Quincy to her birthday party.

"Oh, I gotta go. Our brother is waving me over, probably wanting to introduce me to yet another person. He's been networking from the moment we arrive, and he's forcing me to do the same."

"Aww, it must be rough being you," Tristan cracked and dodged her when she swatted at him. "Make sure you guys stick around. I have a surprise for Cree, and I'd like you two to be here."

Bethany nodded. "I'm sure we will be," she said over her shoulder as she strolled away.

Tristan had just finished his drink when he spotted Nyla heading his way. Apparently, it was time for that surprise.

"You ready?" she asked.

"As ready as I'll ever be."

He followed her, weaving through groups of people until they neared the stage area. He normally didn't play the piano in public, but he thought this would be a fun surprise for Cree. Whenever they stayed at his place, she insisted he play something for her on his baby grand. Now he just hoped he didn't embarrass her or himself when he attempted to play a few songs for her.

Nyla and her husband, Harrison, a talented musician who could play almost every instrument, agreed to help him out. Tristan would play the piano, and Nyla would sing while Harrison played the drums.

When they reached the stage, Harrison was already in position, and Tristan gave him a fist bump before taking a seat at the piano. Suddenly, his nerves were getting the best of him, but he took a deep breath, then released it slowly.

The DJ cut the music when Nyla walked up to the mic. "Excuse me. May I have your attention?" she said and waited for everyone to settle down. "On behalf of my sister and our family, thank you for coming out and celebrating Cree's birthday with us tonight."

Cheers went up around the room, and when Tristan found Cree in the crowd, her eyebrows shot up. He gave her a head nod and grinned. By her surprised expression, it was clear Nyla hadn't told her the plan. Good.

"We have a special treat tonight. In case you didn't know, Tristan Whitmore is in the house!"

More cheers exploded through the space, and it was almost deafening. Tristan stood slightly and gave a wave before he started playing around on the keys.

"Many of you probably know him as a super star football player, but he's so much more. He also has skills on the ivories. Of course, he's not as good as me, but he's not too bad." Everyone laughed before she continued. "But seriously, he's so good on the piano that he decided he wanted to play a few songs for Cree. Isn't that sweet?"

There was laughter and clapping, and once that died down, Tristan glided his fingers over the piano keys, punctuating every note as he started with "Perfect" by Ed Sheeran. He and Harrison did that song as an instrumental, and Nyla didn't sing until Tristan started playing, "I'll Always Love You" by Whitney Houston. It was one of Cree's favorite songs.

His last song, "If I Ain't Got You" by Alicia Keys, was the only one he had actually been planning on playing. As Nyla sang along, her incredible voice as clear as if Alicia Keys was there herself, Tristan closed his eyes and got lost in the melody. The song was a testament of his love for Cree and one of the first songs he learned to play on the piano.

Only a few people knew he had taken piano lessons while

also playing football. He still remembered how he'd wanted to take lessons as a kid, but his parents had barely been able to keep him and his brother in sports. So once he had his own money, and a little free time, he purchased a piano and hired a piano teacher. He currently didn't play as often as he used to, but he was glad he hadn't lost his touch.

When the song ended, he stood and gave a wave and a slight bow. The room exploded in applause. That's when he noticed most people had their phones out taking pictures or maybe even videotaping. It had been awhile since he'd been in the media or saw posts of him on social media. He didn't mind, but he hadn't considered that when he decided to play tonight. He could only imagine what type of comments would come with those posts.

Once the crowd calmed down, Nyla started to speak into the mic, but Tristan stopped her with a hand on her arm. "May I say something?"

She smiled and gestured for him to go ahead. Before he could say a word, someone yelled, "Way to go, Whitmore!" And Tristan laughed.

"Thank you all," he said, still waiting for the room to get a little quieter before saying more.

While he waited, his gaze collided with Cree's, and his heart turned over in his chest. The love glimmering in her gorgeous eyes stoked something so powerful and sensual inside of him. Something Tristan couldn't put a name to, but it was more than love. The sensation was so intense he had to grab on to the mic stand to keep his knees from buckling.

Everything around him disappeared as he only had eyes for Cree. She was a few feet from the stage now, and she had her hand on her chest as she stared at him.

God, this woman...

Tristan felt so blessed to have her in his life, and he fell more in love with her with each passing day. He was looking forward to spending the rest of his life showing her just how much she meant to him, and he was never letting her go.

"She's probably going to kill me for this," he finally said into the mic, "but I'd like for my *wife* to come up on stage."

A gasp sounded from behind him, but Tristan didn't look back at Nyla. His gaze stayed on Cree as quiet murmuring went around the space, people glancing around trying to figure out who he was claiming to be his wife.

When Cree finally moved away from the crowd and headed to the stairs, her guest realized she was the *wife* he was referring to. The room erupted with a chorus of gasps, cheering, screaming, and clapping.

"*Oh my God!*"

"*Whaaat?*"

"*Cree's married?*"

"*You go girl!*"

Seemed everyone was talking at once, but Tristan's attention was only on one person. He moved to the stage's stairs to meet his wife.

My wife, he thought.

He had a wife, a beautiful, sexy, loving wife, and he couldn't help the smile that spread across his mouth when she came into view. Thanks to her, he'd been smiling all the time lately.

"Hey, beautiful." He extended his hand to her, and a sexual charge shot up his arm at her touch. She felt it too if her grin was any indication.

Holding on to him, she carefully climbed the stairs in her sky-high heels. "You were incredible, baby," she said and cupped his cheek before kissing him thoroughly. "Best birthday present ever. Thank you for playing for me."

"My pleasure," he said, and walked hand in hand with her toward the mic.

He wanted to tell the world how much he loved this woman, but he'd start with just telling her friends and family who were in attendance.

They stood at the mic until everyone quieted, and then Tristan lifted his and Cree's joined hands and said, "Years ago, I met a beautiful, sexy, outspoken woman at a night club, and at first, she wouldn't give me no play. I think I asked her to dance, and she said something like, *thanks, but no.*"

Tristan, along with those in the crowd, laughed at the memory.

"But I'm not one for giving up easily. Let's just say, by the time I left that place, I had her telephone number. And that night, after getting home late, I called her and we talked until the wee hours of the morning.

"I knew then she was going to be mine, but if you know Cree, you already know she didn't make it easy. It took awhile for us to get to this point. I'm talking *years!*"

He glanced down at her, and she grinned up at him. Like him, she was probably remembering all that they'd endured during those years, but they made it back to each other.

"I didn't give up, y'all. A week ago, I professed my undying love to her, and then I asked her to marry me. She said yes. Then the other day, we did the deed, and tonight I'd like to introduce you to Mrs. Tristan Whitmore."

Cheers and applause exploded throughout the space, and Tristan pulled Cree into his arms and covered her lips with his. Though he was hungry for so much more than a kiss, he took his time loving on her mouth, soaking up her sweetness as their tongues tangled.

Yes, they didn't get to this moment easily, but Tristan was

confident they'd make it this time. They were going to be okay, and if trouble came their way again, they'd handle it... together.

When the kiss ended, he lowered his forehead to hers. "I love you, baby."

She flashed him a smile that melted his heart. "I love you more, and you're right. We made it."

Nyla approached them first. "I can't believe you got married!" she squealed, and her face broke out into a huge grin. "I'm so happy for you guys! Congratulations, sis!" Then she launched herself at Cree and would've knocked her to the floor if Tristan hadn't been there to catch her.

The sisters hugged and laughed and within seconds, Cree's other siblings, as well as his brother and sister, joined them on stage.

Neither of their parents had been invited to the birthday party since Cree only wanted her siblings and close friends at this event. Tomorrow, he and she planned to share their marriage news with their parents.

"When did you get married?" Dorian asked when she ran onto the stage. But before he or Cree could respond, their siblings started talking at once, throwing out questions and comments faster than they could answer.

"Mom, is going to kill you!"

"I can't believe you're married!"

"Do Mom and Dad know?"

"Oh my God! Mom is going to freak."

"Oh how the mighty have fallen."

Tristan laughed and accepted the hugs and well-wishes.

When Cree had suggested they stay in Atlanta a few extra days, he had no idea she would want to get married while they were there. Though he wanted nothing more than to have her as his wife again, he had tried talking her out of it. He thought, after eloping to Vegas the first time they married, she'd want at least a small wedding with her family this second time around.

She didn't.

She claimed she didn't want the headaches that Dorian was currently experiencing, and then she told him she didn't want to wait. She had said they were going to have some things to deal with regarding her job and maybe media attention, but she didn't care. All she wanted was to be his wife again, and of course he couldn't say no to that.

He wanted to give her whatever she wanted. So, Tristan agreed to marry her in Atlanta by a justice of the peace. That day had been the second-best day of his life, only second to the first time they had gotten married.

Zion pushed past the others and approached Tristan with a huge grin on his face. Tristan started chuckling before Cree's brother uttered a word, knowing it was going to be some nonsense.

"You're a brave man, my brother," Zion said, and they both laughed. "But seriously, dude, welcome to the family."

Chapter Twenty-Seven

Cree snuggled into Tristan, who had his strong arms wrapped around her. They were sitting in a booth at the back of Nyla's club, enjoying a moment together. Months ago, she had started planning her birthday party, never thinking it would be as special as it turned out. That had everything to do with the man who was currently holding her.

Giddiness bubbled inside of Cree as she thought about how he had announced to their friends and family that they were married. They had talked about sharing the news with their siblings tonight, but they hadn't discussed what that would look like.

When Tristan had taken it upon himself to cleverly let the secret out of the bag, then share a little of their story, Cree had fallen harder for him. So used to being the one in charge, coming up with plans and executing them, it felt great not to have to. She loved that she married a man who could take the lead and be in charge, and Tristan had done just that tonight.

She twisted slightly and glanced over her shoulder at him. "You were amazing tonight."

He smirked, flashing those sexy dimples at her. Then he nuzzled her neck while saying, "I think that's what you said to me in bed last night," he cracked, and Cree burst out laughing. What made it even funnier was that she was pretty sure she had said those exact words. Except it was regarding his masterful skills in the bedroom.

"Okay, I can admit you're outstanding in everything you do, but seriously, thank you for playing for me tonight. The song choices you picked were spot on, and I love how you play the piano. I'm thinking you, Nyla, and Harrison can take that act on the road, and I can represent you guys. We could all get paid."

Tristan chuckled and held her closer, and Cree's eyes drifted closed. She basked in his embrace and soaked up the love she could feel pouring from him. Though she was having a good time, and it was great seeing friends and family she hadn't seen in a while, she wouldn't mind cutting her party short. What she really wanted to do was head home and make love with her husband.

My husband.

It was still mind-blowing that she and Tristan had actually gotten married. Again. Just when she thought she'd had her life figured out, the universe threw her a curve ball. And in this case, it was a good one. She felt so blessed and thrilled that Tristan was back and right where he belonged—with her.

Every day, she thanked God for his divine intervention because she never saw this coming. Never imagined she'd be snuggled against the man who she knew was made divinely for her.

As they sat in the booth quietly, they listened to the music pouring through the speakers and the chatter as well as laughter from her guests. She might've been ready to leave, but the party was still going strong. Which meant she needed to get back to mingling with everyone.

Sighing, she said, "I should probably go back and rejoin the party."

"Yeah, considering you're the guest of honor that probably is a good idea," Tristan said as he nibbled on her ear, then placed a gentle kiss against the spot on her neck that always sent tingles through her body. "I'll let you go, but I can't wait to get you home and naked."

Cree laughed as she slowly pulled out of his hold. "I can't wait either. In the meantime, I'll leave you with something to think about."

She kissed him, pouring all the love and admiration she felt for him into the kiss. Tonight felt like the beginning of an amazing life together, and after she finished celebrating her birthday here, she planned on them continuing the celebration at home.

A short while later, as she roamed around the club, greeting and thanking people for attending her party, she spotted Milton watching her. He was near the bar, standing just off to the side, where he could've been easily missed. Knowing the private investigator, she was sure that was intentional.

Cree had sent out invites to the party months ago, and Milton had been on the guest list. Though he had RSVP'd that he'd be there, she hadn't thought about him, especially since she hadn't had any work for him in a while.

She wasn't sure how long he'd been at the party, but she had a feeling he'd been there long enough to know she and Tristan were married.

"Happy birthday, Cree!" two of her college friends said in unison, and they all laughed.

Cree hugged them, thanked them for coming, and when they walked away, she returned her attention to Milton who hadn't moved. He was still watching her, and with a jerk of his head, he nodded toward a hallway. The only thing back there was an entrance to the stage, Nyla's office, and a back exit.

She hoped he wasn't trying to get her to go outside because, as cold as it was out there, that wasn't happening.

She lifted her finger, silently asking for a minute. Since he didn't approach her, Cree could only assume he wanted to talk in private. If that was the case, she wanted to be prepared and went in search of Nyla for the key to her office.

Once that was done, Cree found Milton in the back hall-way, leaning against a wall.

"Hey there," she said. "Thanks for coming to the party. Did you get something to eat and drink?"

"I did, and I am enjoying the celebration. It's been... enlightening. I do have a question, though. What happened to your rule of not mixing business with pleasure? Tristan Whit-more? *Seriously?* I'm a little surprised you hooked up with a client."

Cree didn't like his tone or the disapproving scowl marring his face, but if he had a problem with her and Tristan being together, that was his problem.

"Rules are meant to be broken, and that's one I broke. Any other questions? Comments?" Her tone was hard and unyield-ing, and Cree's invisible claws came out at his mention of Tris-tan. It wasn't her fault if Milton couldn't attract her attention. If he was mad because she never wanted him, oh well. That was his problem too.

Milton didn't say anything for a couple of seconds, and then he chuckled. "You're something else, Cree, but I'm not here to give you shit about your... choices. I'm here because there's something you need to know." He lifted his cell phone. "Is there somewhere private we can talk?"

"That depends. What are we planning to discuss because discussing my *husband* is off limits?"

"Well, let's just say I have information and photos you're going to want to see."

After studying him for a minute, curiosity got the best of Cree, and she led him to Nyla's office. When they entered, she was reminded that her sister's compact workspace was smaller than Cree's walk-in closet, but it didn't matter. She didn't intend on being in there long.

She propped herself on the edge of the desk and folded her arms across her chest. She didn't miss the way Milton's gaze traveled to her breasts, lingered, and then returned to her face.

Struggling not to roll her eyes, she said, "Okay talk. What's so important that you had to bring it to my attention tonight of all nights?"

Milton cleared his throat. "A couple of hours ago, a friend of mine, another private investigator, told me someone at your firm hired him to follow you."

Unease crept through Cree, and she slowly pushed away from the desk. "What are you talking about?"

"The only reason I'm even bringing this to your attention is because I consider us friends," he said as he pulled something up on his phone. "I don't know what's going on at the firm, but someone is digging into your life."

"Who?"

"My contact wouldn't say who, but he knows I've done a lot of work for you, and he gave me a courtesy call. When he turns in his report to his client, it will include photos, as well as information that he's found on you."

Milton handed her his phone, and Cree glanced at the screen. As she sifted through photos of her and Tristan, confusion and anger battled within her. Some pictures were from as early as the day she met Tristan at the condo near the lakefront.

Others included them leaving the grocery store, kissing outside of a restaurant, and there was even a picture of them as recent as yesterday, standing in front of the commercial building Tristan had just purchased.

What Cree didn't see were any photos of her and Tristan in Atlanta. That didn't mean they didn't exist. The more photos she viewed, cataloging her and her husband's relationship, the madder she got.

Whoever the PI was, he'd been following her for a while without her knowing, which was disturbing. But why? Why would someone at the firm hire a private investigator to follow her?

As she pondered the question, she thought about her conversations with Warren. Of course, he was the first person to come to mind. She got along well with Felicia Watts, the other partner of the firm, as well as their associate lawyers.

But Warren? From the moment he had questioned the contract she had signed with Tristan, curious about why it was only for six months, he'd been acting strangely around her. Then again, if she was honest, he'd been treating her differently for longer than that. They used to work well together. Yet for the last few months, she felt he was in competition with her. After she'd signed Tristan, the tension between them grew, and he questioned almost everything she did. But why?

As she paced in a small circle, one question after another bombarded her mind. Was Warren planning to use the photos against her somehow? He might know she and Tristan were married. Did he intend to put her on blast with her other clients? Have them questioning her integrity and ethics?

She stopped and looked at Milton. "Why are you giving me a heads-up on this?" she asked as she handed him his phone.

"I told you because we're friends."

Cree studied him for a few minutes, searching his eyes,

questioning if he was being honest. At first, she wondered why he hadn't been the one hired to follow her, but she knew why. The people she worked with knew she and Milton were friendly. They wouldn't have hired him to do their dirty work, knowing there was a chance he'd tell her what was going on.

"I'm serious, Cree. Just because you've turned down my advances doesn't mean I don't still consider you a friend. There are no hard feelings, and I only brought this to you with good intentions. Oh, and congratulations on your marriage. I'm not sure if I mentioned that."

"Everything okay in here?"

Cree jerked her head to the open door to find Tristan standing there looking fierce and intimidating. She had momentarily forgotten about the party, even though she could still hear the music and her guests in the distance.

Her husband's gaze moved from her to Milton and then back to her again before he entered the room like he owned the space. Her heart rate increased. Her pulse pounded in her ear. And her girlie parts sparked with awareness.

He'd always had a visceral effect on her, and now that they were married, her body lit up from the inside out whenever she was in his presence.

When he stopped in front of her, and slid his arm around her waist, Cree didn't miss the concern in his eyes.

"What's going on in here? You okay?"

She nodded. "Yeah, baby, I'm fine, but we have a situation."

Chapter Twenty-Eight

L ong after the party was over and they were back at Cree's place, Tristan couldn't stop thinking about the conversation in Nyla's office. When he'd been searching around for her during the party, Nyla had been the one to tell him where she was.

Tristan had gone looking for his wife, thinking she might've been sick or something since Nyla hadn't known why she'd needed the office. What he hadn't expected to find was her in there with Milton. It was a good thing they'd left the door open. Otherwise, Tristan probably would've jumped to the wrong conclusion despite trusting Cree.

Who he didn't trust was Milton. It didn't take a genius to know the private investigator was attracted to Cree. Who wouldn't be? His wife was sexy as hell and attracted attention from the opposite sex like honey attracted bees.

Tristan had witnessed the man's appreciative glances at Cree the first time they saw each other in her office. Cree assured him there was nothing going on between them. But tonight, for a brief moment, Tristan had wondered if that was still true.

Cree quickly cleared up any misconceptions when she explained why she'd been meeting with Milton in private. Now all Tristan could think about was whether she was in danger. He found it hard to believe a partner at her firm was having someone spy on her. The pictures were disturbing and invasive. The worst part? Neither of them realized anyone had been following them. Tristan was sure that going forward they'd be more aware of their surroundings.

But why had Warren, who Cree suspected of being behind this, wanted to spy on her? What was he looking for? Cree insisted she would talk to the guy Monday, but Tristan wanted to hunt the bastard down tonight and get answers.

"Sweetheart, it's almost three o'clock in the morning," Tristan said as he released a loud yawn. "Can't whatever you're doing wait until the sun comes up?"

He was lounging on the sofa in her home office while she was sitting at her desk going through documents. Every so often, she'd take notes on her legal pad but then go right back to reading.

She glanced up and looked at him. Considering he was crazy tired, she looked like she was getting her second wind. She had dozed off for about twenty minutes while he drove them back to his place, but the moment he pulled into her parking spot, she'd been wide awake.

"I could wait, but I want to take advantage of being pissed off. I work better when I'm in the mood to rip someone's throat out, and let's just say Warren is lucky he's not here."

Tristan snorted and went to her. "But you don't know yet if he's behind any of this."

"I'd bet a year's salary that it's him, and I'm going to get him to admit to it."

When she went back to reading, Tristan positioned himself between her and the desk, nudging her chair back in the process. Which also forced her to set down the papers.

"Tristan," she whined.

Now that he was closer, he could see she was just as tired as he was. Shortly after arriving, he had showered and climbed into bed, thinking she would do the same. But after falling asleep while she went through her nightly routine, Tristan had awakened to find her side of the bed empty. She hadn't been to bed at all, and this was where he'd found her.

His gaze raked over the light blue lounge set she was wearing. The top was baggy with long sleeves and a very deep vee in the front, and his body stirred at the way her pert nipples pushed against the garment.

As exhausted as he was, he should be too tired to make love to her, but Cree had a way of keeping him turned on. Even more so considering the way she was currently checking him out. Her hungry gaze was taking in his bare, muscular chest, and he smiled.

She had a love-hate thing going when he roamed around the house shirtless, especially if she was trying to get work done, like now.

"Dammit, Tristan." She rolled her chair forward and wrapped her arms around his waist, then placed a lingering kiss near his navel and just above the waistband of his lounge pants.

His dick twitched, and he groaned. "Now you're playing with fire. Don't start nothing you ain't planning to finish."

After a slight hesitation, she chuckled and dropped back in her seat. "You're so damn tempting, but I need to go through every line of this contract before I talk to my lawyer in the morning." She glanced around him at the clock on the laptop, then sat back again. "Well, considering it's already morning, I'll be talking with her in a few hours."

"On a Sunday?" Tristan asked.

Cree nodded. "I made a decision. I'm leaving the firm, but it's not as easy as handing in a letter of resignation. Since I'm a partner, I technically need to give a sixty-day notice. Which I actually thought was ninety days, but after going through that portion of the contract, it's only sixty. Still, if I don't like what Warren has to say when I confront him Monday, I need to be prepared to walk away."

She explained the complexity of dissolving the contract between her and the firm. Especially if she ended up leaving with short notice, like she was planning. It was clear this was something she'd been thinking about doing, but not this soon and not because some asshole had hired a private investigator to tail her.

Listening to her talk about all that would need to happen before she could leave, Tristan was thinking it might actually take those ninety days to wrap everything up. There was a lot to take into consideration, especially when it came to her clients and transitioning them. At least those who would be interested in following her. Just because she could take them with her, there were steps the firm required in doing that.

At some point, there would also have to be an emergency meeting called between her, Warren, and their other partner, Felicia Watts, which posed a problem. Watts was on medical leave, and though Cree hoped the woman would be able to do a virtual meeting, she wasn't sure that would happen.

Cree also had to be prepared financially to cover her portion of liabilities and any fees attached to her breaking the contract. As she ticked off one step after another that would need to take place, Tristan's admiration for her spiked. He had always loved her brain and was fascinated in how quickly her mind worked.

"I'm glad you're ready to go out on your own. You have an

office you can move into whenever you're ready, and you already know I'll be right there with you every step of the way," he said, brushing her long bang away from her eyes. "Also, if you have to buy your way out of the firm, we can do that. I've already added you to all my bank accounts. So use the money, Cree. Whatever you need to do to get your freedom."

She shook her head. "I'm not using your money," she said with finality.

Tristan growled under his breath. He was too tired to argue with her about this again. They had already had a major blowup before they got married because she had wanted him to have a prenup drawn up. He thought the idea was ludicrous and had explained that whatever was his was hers. He meant that despite her objections.

As far as he was concerned, he owed her, and when he told her that, she had gotten even angrier, claiming he didn't owe her anything.

Of course, he saw the situation differently. She hadn't accepted anything when they divorced the last time, and he would've given her the world if she'd wanted it. She couldn't seem to understand that he credited her with him even being able to accomplish his dream of playing in the NFL. Why couldn't she see that he wanted to share all that he had accomplished and accumulated with her?

"Cree," he said, but he was too tired to say more.

He was still propped against the edge of her desk, and she stood, wrapping her arms around his neck.

"I love you, and I'm so grateful to have you as my husband. I don't want us to argue but just knowing you have my back means everything to me, Tristan. And don't worry, I'll probably eventually spend your money." She smiled and kissed him. "You just make sure you're ready to fund any retail therapy I might need after I finish dealing with Warren, okay?"

Tristan pressed his lips to hers for a quick kiss. "All right."

He didn't want to argue either, and as long as she knew she could count on him, everything else would work itself out. He just hoped she got the results she wanted after her talk with Warren. Otherwise, Tristan might have to pay the guy a visit himself.

Chapter Twenty-Nine

Cree paced the length of her office, her feet quiet against the plush carpet. From the moment she arrived at the firm, she debated on whether her plan of confronting Warren was a good one.

What if he wasn't the person who hired the PI? But each time that thought flashed through her mind, she shot it down. He had to be the one behind all this, and instead of waiting to play defense, she was playing offense.

She stopped near the window and stared out at nothing in particular as she thought about the private investigator. Cree wasn't sure when he was turning in his report, but she had a feeling it would be soon. Otherwise, the guy probably wouldn't have shared anything with Milton the other day, but she couldn't be sure.

What concerned Cree most was not knowing what was in the report. The photos were damning, clearly showing her dating her client, but what else would the PI share?

Sighing, she thought about something else that came up yesterday. She and Tristan had spent part of the day before looking at social media posts of those who had attended her party. There were videos of Tristan playing the piano, and tons of photos that included the two of them together. More importantly, the news was getting around about their marriage.

Maybe they shouldn't have been so rash in eloping without thinking everything through. But Cree hadn't been able to help herself. Being in love with Tristan was all-consuming, and it was easy to throw caution to the wind when your man made you feel like all was well in the world.

She soon found out it wasn't when her parents called before she and Tristan could share the news. To say Virginia was disappointed was an understatement. She dreamed of planning weddings for all her girls, and she told Cree that she robbed her of doing just that. Her mother also insisted Cree's father was looking forward to one day walking her down the aisle.

Virginia had always been good at laying on the guilt. The only thing that saved the conversation from being too disappointing was when Tristan told both sets of parents that he and Cree were planning a reception for family and their closest friends. That appeased everyone, and the best part was Cree didn't have to plan it. They immediately hired a wedding planner with specific instructions on what they wanted and didn't want. The number one item—guests. No more than a hundred.

In the meantime, Cree needed to focus on her career.

Huffing out a cleansing breath, she strolled out of her office. It was time for a face-to-face with Warren. Wearing a double-breasted suit dress that hugged all her curves and stopped just above her knees, Cree felt powerful and in charge. Not only did the outfit catch attention, but it made her feel like the badass Tristan claimed her to be.

As she approached Warren's closed office door, she slowed

and mentally thought about everything she needed to say to him. Once she was ready, she gave the door a quick knock, and then she did something he often did, she walked in like she owned the place.

Warren was seated at his desk but stood abruptly, confusion on his face. "Cree. Since when do you barge into my office?"

She closed the door and approached his desk. "Since you decided it was a good idea to have me followed. Did you honestly think I wouldn't find out that you hired a private investigator to keep tabs on me?"

Though she didn't know for sure if Warren was behind this, Cree was taking a gamble. She couldn't think of anyone else at the firm who would do something like this, and she watched Warren carefully for any signs of deception.

He removed his readers and set them on the desk, giving her a better view of his deep gray unflinching eyes. His salt and pepper, full mane of hair had recently been cut and was as neat as usual. He believed in looking his best, and the expensive three-piece suit, that draped perfectly over his slim build, was a testament to that fact.

"I don't know what you're talking about," he said and reclaimed his seat. He opened a file folder on his desk and started to look through it.

Seriously?

Cree slammed the folder shut. No way was she going to stand there and be ignored.

Warren shot up out of his desk chair again and glared at her. "Now you wait just one minute! You can't come into my office and accuse me of anything. I told you I don't know what you're talking about."

"And I think you do!" she snapped, anger hanging on the

fringes of her control, especially when she knew for sure he was lying.

Warren had a tell. His left eye twitched when he wasn't being completely honest. She'd first noticed it a few months after joining the firm. It was such a small flicker that, if someone wasn't paying attention, they'd miss it.

"What I don't know is why? So, I suggest you start talking before I really get mad. Why did you hire a private investigator to follow me around?"

"I told you. I don't know what you're talking..."

Cree slammed the side of her fist on his desk, causing several items to jostle. "Dammit, Warren! I'm not playing games here. I want the truth, and I want it now."

He released a humorless laugh as he walked around his desk, stopping a few feet from her. "You want the truth? Why don't you start by telling me about how you dated, maybe fucked, and then married one of our clients. It's amazing the things you can learn while watching a sports news channel.

"Imagine my surprise while watching football recaps last night, a sports analyst mentioned Tristan Whitmore got married. Not just married but married to one of our attorneys!" he roared.

Cree sighed and debated on how to respond. She knew that topic would come up at some point, but she wasn't going to let him deflect.

"You answer my questions, then I'll answer yours," she said simply. "Why did you send a private investigator after me?"

After staring her down, Warren grumbled something under his breath. "I did hire a private investigator," he said as he reclaimed his seat.

Cree leaned on the back of one of the guest chairs that faced his desk. "Why? What were you after, Warren? Are you so jealous of my success that you have to dig up dirt to try to make me look bad?"

"I did it to protect the interest of this firm. This place will always be my top priority."

"And mine too."

"Is it though? First, you only sign Whitmore to a six-month contract, which is unheard of around here. Especially for a high-profile client. Then when I questioned you about it, you got cagey."

"What are you talking about? I told you Tristan and I had history. I wanted to see if we could work together again, and we both agreed a short contract to start with would be in our best interest. But if we're being honest here, Warren, you've been treating me strangely for months."

He shrugged. "I was concerned you were doing something underhanded that could affect the firm, and I was right. Dating a client is taboo, but you know that. You should've handed his account over to one of us the moment you even thought about screwing around with Whitmore," he said with disgust. "Where's your integrity? You could get sanctioned or maybe even disbarred for dating a client."

"The latter won't happen since me and Mr. Whitmore had a relationship before I became his lawyer."

"What? That three-day marriage thirteen years ago? That's beside the point. You knowingly dated one of the firm's clients, and discipline actions will be taken."

Anger boiled inside of Cree. At least now she knew the PI was thorough. "Did you hire a private investigator to dig up dirt on me so you can have me fired or, worse, disbarred? Is it your intention to sabotage my career?"

"What?" he asked, faking concern. "How could you even think that? I'm just looking out for the firm I started."

"And how could you think I'd do anything to intentionally sabotage the firm?" she countered.

Yes, it was unethical to date Tristan, but she married him in a short period of time before anyone, except Warren and his PI, knew. If he did try to go after her license, she could argue she and Tristan had a previous relationship before he signed with the firm. That would make a difference in the eyes of the law, especially since they were once married and now remarried.

Cree wanted to wipe the smug look off his face. "What else do your PI dig up?"

"Question is what should we do about this situation? I saw on the partners' group calendar that you set up an emergency meeting for this afternoon. You beat me to it. I received the report from the private investigator yesterday and..." His voice trailed off, and he narrowed his eyes at her. "How did you know I hired a PI?"

Cree stood upright and folded her arms across her chest as she looked down at him. "My husband is a very wealthy man with connections you and I could only dream of," she said, partly lying but going with it. She didn't want anything to come back on Milton or his PI contact. "It's such a small world, Warren. You never know who knows who."

"What's that supposed to mean?"

Instead of answering, she said, "Since it's clear you want me out of here, I'm going to give you what you want. We can start the dissolution process. I'm hoping we can settle everything within thirty days instead of sixty. I think it would be in all our best interest if I leave the firm."

"It's not that easy. There will be a lot to settle, debts to take care of, and—"

"I will pay whatever it takes for a speedy dissolution and to be free and clear of the firm. All I ask is that you keep your mouth closed about your PI's findings, and you give me a copy of his or her report."

Warren burst out laughing as he swiveled back and forth in his chair. "Why would I do that? I have enough information on you to start disciplinary actions, and if I wanted to, I probably could go a step further. Maybe talk with the courts about your sexual misconduct. You know—because you dating a client is highly unethical."

"It was unethical for you to hire a PI to follow me around and dig into my life for no good reason," Cree said, even if he did have a fairly good reason. "If you wanted to know something about me, you could've asked. I would have answered your questions, and like you, I care about this firm. I have brought in a ton of money that shows just how much I care. It's a shame it has to end like this with you trying to sabotage me."

"What's a shame is that you put the reputation of this firm at risk!" he snapped.

Cree remained silent because he was right. She could admit that to herself. She should've handled the situation with Tristan better. Mainly, she should've transferred his account to someone else or waited until the six months were up before hooking up with him. But it was too late for that. Still, she didn't like how smug Warren was being about this.

And before she could stop herself, she said, "How would you feel knowing the private investigator I hired to look into *you* gave me some damning information? I wonder how your wife would react if I shared the findings with her."

Cree could honestly say she had never seen blood drain from a person's face. Warren suddenly turned white, and he swallowed hard as his chest heaved.

Interesting. She was bluffing, taking a chance that he had something to hide and apparently, he did. Maybe the rumors years ago, before she joined the firm, were true.

Cree had heard one of the firm's associates had accused him of sexual assault. The woman had retracted her claim almost immediately, quit the firm, and the situation went away quietly. Cree wouldn't be surprised if Warren had paid her off. She also wouldn't be surprised if he had plenty of other things to hide. By his weary expression, her guess would be he did.

He stood slowly from his seat, no longer wearing the smug expression from moments ago. Instead, he looked like he wanted to pummel her. "Are you threatening me?" he asked.

"Not at all," Cree said, standing her ground. "I'm just saying two can play the same games. Glass houses, Warren. Glass houses."

She glanced down and picked invisible lent off her dress before looking at him again. "Now that we have an understanding, we can get to work on the dissolution process. The sooner we do, the sooner you'll be rid of me."

Chapter Thirty

"**D**ude, can you sit down somewhere? You've been pacing for what seems like hours," Quincy said, and Tristan stopped and glared at him.

"I've only been here twenty minutes. How could I be pacing for hours?" he shot back.

Tristan didn't bother telling his brother that he'd been pacing at home initially but started getting on his own nerves and had to get some air. That's how he ended up at the commercial building that he had recently purchased. He thought stopping by there would help take his mind off Cree.

It hadn't.

He was anxious to hear how the conversation with Warren had gone. Since she'd been planning on talking with him first thing that morning, Tristan thought he would've heard from her by now. It was after two, and he had texted her to check in, but he'd gotten radio silence.

Worried something might've happened, he had even called the receptionist to find out if she had even made it into the office. Shantel told him Cree was in the building, but she'd had back-to-back meetings.

Before Tristan stopped by the new offices for the nonprofit, he'd gone by the office space that Cree had identified she wanted. It wasn't as big as the office suite on the top floor, the one that used to have a law office tenant, but it was big enough for her and a few support staff. Which was what she said she wanted. Though it would be awhile before Cree moved in, he'd been glad to see that it had been totally cleaned out.

"So, what's going on? Clearly there's something on your mind," Quincy said, pulling Tristan out of his thoughts. "Oh wait. Is it Mom and Dad? I heard Mom had given you an earful for eloping."

"Yeah," Tristan said and sat in the chair next to Quincy's desk. The movers had moved boxes and all the furniture for the nonprofit to the new building, and his brother was unpacking.

"Yeah, Mom let us have it. She's thrilled to have another daughter, but she was pissed they didn't get to be a part of our wedding day. She had hoped by now at least one of her kids would've had a wedding."

Quincy chuckled. "Imagine if she knew she had missed two of your weddings."

Again, Tristan found himself glowering at his brother. "I don't know why you're laughing. You're the oldest. She should be looking at you to finally get married and have a big wedding."

Quincy shrugged. "When my Mrs. Right comes along, maybe I'll do just that. Until then, I'm going to continue having a good time out here enjoying the bachelor's life."

That was one thing Tristan didn't miss. After being in a relationship with Cree, he'd known immediately he didn't want to be single. He was a relationship kind of guy and didn't like yo-yo dating. The years he and Cree were divorced had been awful, especially when women practically threw themselves at him.

It might not have been so bad if he'd been interested, but none of them were Cree. The one time he did try a relationship again, it was so unfulfilling that it just left him and the woman disappointed.

"I suggested to Mom that, if she wanted a wedding, maybe she should help you and Bethany find a mate."

Quincy's head jerked up from the folders he was organizing. "You didn't!"

Tristan laughed for the first time that day. "Actually, I did. I told her that Cree's mom has been trying to matchmake her kids for years, and four out of five of them are married. I also told her that Mrs. Priestly has several grandchildren."

"Dammit, Tristan! That's why she probably left me that voicemail inviting me over to dinner Friday night. She claimed there's some people she wants me to meet who are interested in the nonprofit. That's a first for her, and now I know why."

Tristan burst out laughing. He just had that conversation with their mother the day before. "Man, Mom works fast."

"I can't believe you, man. I've always looked out for you, and this is how you treat me?"

Quincy looked so bereft, Tristan tried not to laugh, but he couldn't stop the snicker. His brother was right, he had always looked out for Tristan, coming through for him more times than he could count.

"I'm sorry, Quincy. I had no idea she'd take my suggestion, but would it be so bad if she found you a woman?" When Quincy shot him an incredulous look, Tristan lifted his hands. "Hear me out. You're not getting any younger. Don't you want children? You don't want to be that guy at fifty with a toddler and—"

"Dude, I'm not even forty yet. I have time, but all that is beside the point. Would you want Mom finding you a woman?"

"No," he answered honestly. "I'm sorry. Hopefully after you tell Mom to back off, she'll listen. Or you can always sick her on Bethany. It wouldn't hurt for our sister to get hooked up with a good man."

Before Quincy could respond, Tristan's phone buzzed in his pants pocket, and he hurried and pulled it out. He hoped it was Cree, but a glance at the screen showed it was his real estate agent calling.

"Hello."

"Hi Tristan, I'm glad I caught you. I think I found the perfect home for you and Cree."

Tristan listened as she spouted off the highlights of the home, including that it was in one of Cree's chosen suburbs. It had the number of bedrooms and bathrooms they were looking for, as well as a pool and pool house. The two-car attached garage and a three-car standalone garage were perfect. That's where most of the homes he'd looked at lately had fallen short.

"Any chance you guys are able to take a look at this gorgeous home today? It's move-in ready, and the seller is very motivated."

Tristan glanced at the time, wondering when he'd hear from Cree. "Cathy, I'm not sure. I'd have to check with my wife and get back to you. Are there any other homes in the area that fit what we're looking for?"

"There was one more a few blocks away from this one, but I heard this morning that the owners accepted an offer. I'll keep looking, but Tristan I think this one is the one. If there's any chance you two can meet me there today, just give me a call back."

"Cathy found another house for you to look at?" Quincy asked when Tristan disconnected the call.

"Yeah, it sounds like a good contender. Hopefully, it's all she says it is because I'm tired of looking."

He was so ready to find their dream home and get settled in. They had hoped that would happen before Thanksgiving, but seeing the holiday was next week, Tristan had given up hope. But if they could find a place and get moved in by Christmas, that would be great too. He felt once they were in one place, instead of bouncing between their two condos, he'd feel a bit more settled. Then they could start planning the rest of their life.

Quincy stood. "I need to go downstairs and talk with one of the tenants in the building. You gonna still be here when I return?"

"Probably not. I'm going to head out soon."

"Okay, lock up when you leave, and I'll catch you later."

"Will do."

Tristan's phone rang, and when he realized it was Cree, he answered quickly.

"Hey, baby."

"Hey yourself."

Relief flooded through Tristan at hearing her voice. "How'd it go with Warren?"

"Things started... interestingly, but once Warren and I came to an understanding, we were prepared to meet with Felicia. After long discussions and hashing out a few important issues, I'll get what I want... at a cost. But I'll tell you all about that when I see you."

"Okay," he said slowly, hearing something else in her voice, maybe weariness. "You don't sound good. You okay? Are you ready for me to come get you?"

He had dropped her off that morning, but she thought it best if he was not seen there until after she talked with Warren.

"I'm fine. Just a little tired, and anxious to see you. Instead of you picking me up, I'll get a car and come to you. Where are you?"

"At the commercial building. Are you sure you don't want me to come get you?"

"No, that's okay. I think it'll be better if you stay clear of the offices here. I'll come to you. Or I can meet you at home. Umm, your condo."

That was a reminder that they needed to find *their* home.

"Are you too tired to go look at a house?"

He told her what little he knew about the place and how Cathy insisted it ticked off all the boxes on their long list of must haves.

"It sounds perfect, and if it's as great as she says, others will be looking at it too," Cree said. "Let's get something to eat and then go check out the house."

"Okay, baby. I'll have something here for you to eat, and then we can head to Wilmette."

"All right. See you soon."

* * *

Two hours later, as Cree rode in the passenger seat while Tristan drove them to the house, she felt almost human again. She'd been dead on her feet when leaving the office, feeling as if she didn't have enough energy to think, let alone walk out the door.

But after eating and then going back to Tristan's place to change into something more comfortable, she felt like herself. During the ride to the house, she'd been telling Tristan about her meeting with Warren. Cree didn't miss the way her husband's hands had tightened on the steering wheel during certain parts of the story.

He seemed to relax a little when she told him that she and

Warren had agreed to sign an NDA regarding information that the PIs shared. Tristan laughed awhile about how she had bluffed about having had Warren investigated. Cree had been surprised he hadn't asked for proof. Maybe because she hadn't pushed to see the report he had received from his PI. Cree was glad that part worked out, and they agreed Felicia and no one else needed to know about that particular agreement.

Tristan reached over and linked his fingers with hers as he divided his attention between her and the highway. "Do you think it will take as long as you originally thought to be totally done with the firm?"

"No, I'll pay the agreed-upon fees for breaking the contract. I'll also need to cover my share of liabilities and the firm's debts, and then I also offered to pay what the three of us are calling incidental fees.

"I'm taking ownership of the fact that I was in the wrong for dating a client. Though I know you wouldn't have sued us or somehow made trouble for the firm," she said to Tristan. "I did put the company at risk. So that was on me. I made a financial offer, and the partners accepted. But it'll probably still take at least forty-five to sixty days to take care of everything."

She intended to work mostly outside of the office but planned to show up in person for any necessary meetings. She also had some vacation time which she would use between the Thanksgiving holiday and New Year's Day. Which was another reason she hoped they found a house soon. It would be great to have time off while she and Tristan got settled into their new home.

"What about your clients?" Tristan asked.

"I'll be taking those who are interested in moving with me. All in all, I'm happy things turned out as well as they did."

A few minutes later, Tristan found the block where the home was located, and Cree smiled as they drove along the cobblestone, treelined street. Excitement sprang to life inside of her. The peacefulness of the area was felt as they drove slowly, taking in well-maintained yards and passing one beautiful home after the next.

When Tristan reached the front of the property, they stared out at it, taking it all in. The real estate agent mentioned the owner had purchased the adjacent land years ago, and now the stately home sat on two lots with a huge yard surrounding it.

A big yard had been one of the items on Tristan's revised-home-buying wish list, second to five garage stalls.

"We'll have to get a better fence because this one doesn't offer any security," he said of the white picket fence as he drove slowly up the driveway. "I want us to have an eight-foot wrought-iron fence around the entire property, and a double-hung gate and call box installed at the entrance."

As Tristan thought about security, Cree's attention was on the professionally done landscape. Statuesque trees were perfectly placed around the yard, and a three-tiered lighted fountain was positioned near the front of the house. Flower and rock beds, as well as various sized shrubbery were strategically placed.

This is it, a small voice said inside Cree's head as the home came fully into view. This could possibly be the house they raise their family in.

Tristan parked in front of the garage next to Cathy's vehicle. When they both climbed out of his sports car, Tristan held Cree's hand while they stood outside the home. The structure was made up of white painted brick and some other type of material Cree couldn't identify. She loved how the black trim made the house look modern, but still homey. There were also a ton of windows, which she appreciated.

Cathy opened the front door with a cell phone to her ear

and her hand over the mouthpiece. "Come on in and look around. I'll be right with you."

When Cree and Tristan entered the home, they stood in the grand foyer and glanced around. Straight ahead was the large living room with a breathtaking fireplace taking center stage. To the left of it was a wall of windows that overlooked a deck and yard. They both loved open floor plans, and a portion of the kitchen could be seen just off the living room.

For Cree, it felt like home and she hadn't even seen the whole place.

She looked at Tristan just as he turned to glance at her, and he smiled.

Oh good. He feels it too.

Wrapping his arm around her shoulder, he pulled her to his side and kissed the top of her head. "Well, Mrs. Whitmore, this might be the beginning of the rest of our lives."

Cree chuckled as giddiness bubbled inside of her. The last few months had been like a fantasy that she hadn't dared to ever dream. The love of her life was back, they were married, and she was on the brink of starting her own law firm.

And now this. They might have found their forever home.

Her heart was so full, she was afraid it would burst from her chest.

"Thank you, Tristan," she whispered.

He frowned down at her. "For what?"

"For not giving up on us, and for following through on that *Win-Cree-Back* plan you told me about." They both laughed. "More than any of that, though, thank you for loving me."

"Always, baby. I will always love you."

Epilogue

 *month later...*

"We survived our first Christmas with the family," Cree said as she dropped down on the sofa next to Tristan. "And I feel like I've been running a mile a minute for the last two weeks."

Tristan chuckled. A glass of bourbon was in one of his hands, and he draped his other arm around her shoulders. "To say the weeks since moving into our home have been eventful, would be an understatement. But I have to admit, this has been the best Christmas I've ever had thanks to you."

Cree smiled and snuggled closer. She felt the same way.

They were sitting on the sofa facing the fireplace, and she marveled at how Christmasy everything looked. The crackling fire, the humongous Christmas tree her husband insisted they needed, and the twinkling lights in every single window, made their new home look festive and feel warm and inviting.

As the real estate agent had predicted before showing them the place, they had immediately fallen in love with the home. They had put an offer in on the spot, willing to pay cash, and their offer had been accepted within a few minutes.

From there, the days had flown by. Not only did they buy a house, but they had to pack up Cree's place, organize movers, and take care of a host of other tasks. They also had a wedding reception the weekend after Thanksgiving.

The reception hadn't been as grand as their mothers had wanted, but Cree thought the cookout at her in-law's new home had been perfect. It had been too cold to hang outside, but there had been more than enough space for their friends and family to congregate indoors.

Then, two weeks ago, she and Tristan had moved into their forever home. It hadn't taken long for her condo to sell, and they decided to hold on to Tristan's condo for a little while. The idea of having a place in town appealed to them both, but Cree doubted they'd stay there often, if at all. They both were in love with this place.

The eight bedrooms and eight-in-half bathrooms was extreme, but they wanted a place that could hold family and friends whenever they visited. All the bedrooms weren't decorated, and they hadn't hung all the pictures or unpacked all her boxes, but today it had served its purpose. Both sides of the family had spent the day with them eating, drinking, playing games, and enjoying each other.

"Yep, best Christmas ever," Tristan murmured as if reading her mind. "I think we should host Christmas every year."

"I could get with that," Cree agreed. "Especially if it's like this year where I didn't have to do much."

The women in the family pulled together and cooked a feast, and having a kitchen large enough for all of them to fit had been a bonus.

"Did you hear everyone talking about my amazing Christmas decorations?" Tristan asked. "My skills are endless."

Cree chuckled. "Don't you mean the Christmas interior designer skills are endless?"

"I said what I said. Who do you think gave her all the ideas? Like the garland and twinkling lights above the windows, and that big, twenty-foot tree in the corner—sparkling like diamonds under a spotlight—that was all me.

"And don't forget about those poinsettias on either side of the fireplace," he said, nodding at the beautiful plants, "and the one on the dining room table—all me. The Christmas themed bathroom down the hall? *Me.* That's only half of what I told her we wanted. So yeah, I'm taking full credit."

Cree shook her head and laughed. "How did I not know you were obsessed with Christmas?"

"I don't know because it's been my favorite holiday since I was a kid. Maybe you never knew because when we first met, I barely had two nickels to rub together. Decorating for Christmas was out of the question. Now that we have a little money, there are some things I want us to splurge on."

"Like more Christmas decorations?" she asked and smiled.

"Exactly."

For the next few minutes they sat in silence, each lost in their own thoughts. It had been a long day, but as Cree remembered bits and pieces of it, she couldn't help but feel joy at being able to spend time with their family. The day had truly been story-book worthy and something she would never forget.

"Something else I think we should add to our new list of traditions is the family singing Christmas carols around the piano," Tristan said, and once again, Cree had to agree.

They had so much space in the house, Tristan had converted one of the large bedrooms on the first floor into a piano room. His baby grand sat in the middle of the floor, and along the perimeter of the space was comfortable seating for at least thirty people.

"You and Nyla leading a round of Christmas carols was one of the highlights of the day," Cree said. Her sister had a beautiful singing voice and had sat next to Tristan on the piano bench while he played one song after another. Tristan's musical talent on the piano never ceased to amaze Cree, and she could listen to him play all day every day.

Tristan drained his glass and said, "Are you ready to head up to bed?"

Cree nodded. "Yes. I'm wiped out, but there's something I need your help with in the bedroom."

Tristan laughed and gave her a quick kiss on the lips. "I do love the way you think, and I'm always willing to help fulfill your needs."

Cree laughed and stood.

After tidying up downstairs and making sure the house was locked up for the night, they headed upstairs hand in hand. When they reached the bedroom, Tristan started undressing, and Cree went into the bathroom.

Her heart started beating double-time and anxiousness swirled within her like a flock of birds taking flight inside her gut. She grabbed the small paper bag from under her sink that she had placed there a few days ago and returned to the bedroom.

"Something else I was..." Tristan started but stopped when he spotted her standing in the doorway of the bathroom. Cree wasn't sure what he saw on her face, but in two steps, he was in front of her.

"What's wrong?" he asked in a rush, cupping her face between his large hands. "Are you feeling okay?"

Cree released a long breath and held up the paper bag before holding it out to him.

His eyebrows dipped into a frown as he took the bag. "What's this?" When he looked inside, he started to say more but froze. Seconds ticked by before he glanced at her. "Are you... Does this mean... umm..." he stuttered, and Cree laughed.

"I don't know for sure, but I thought tonight we can see if we're pregnant."

Tristan just stared at her, his chest heaving and a range of emotions flashed across his face. They both had agreed they wanted to start trying for a baby right away, even though they both held concerns. After Cree's miscarriage, the doctor had assured her that there was no reason why she shouldn't be able to carry future babies to full term. But of course, she couldn't stop the fear of losing another child from creeping into her mind.

The other day, when she realized she was two weeks late when normally her cycle was like clockwork, she decided to buy a pregnancy test. Her problem was, she hadn't decided when to tell Tristan. At first, she considered taking the test and only mentioning it to him if it turned up positive, but she quickly shot that idea down. He had missed out on everything centered around her previous pregnancy, and she vowed to never let that happen again.

"That's why you've been turning down alcohol this past week," Tristan said more to himself, still looking a little dazed.

"Yeah, I figured I'd better be safe than sorry. Okay, so I'm going in here to do my part," she said pointing to the bathroom, "but I'll need you when it's time to look at the results."

Tristan nodded, then cupped her face between his hands again and kissed her. "I'll be right here. Whatever the results, just remember we're in this together... forever."

Cree nodded, struggling to keep her emotions in check. Part of her was excited about the possibility, but the other part of her didn't want to be disappointed. Not with the results and not with the chance of another miscarriage. More than anything, she didn't want to disappoint Tristan. He wanted a family just as much as she did.

A few minutes later, Cree exited the bathroom, her hands shaking. They had to wait a few minutes before they'd know, and her nerves were on edge.

"Come here," Tristan said, pulling her into one of his famous bear hugs. "How are you feeling?"

"I don't know. I'm excited and nervous, while also being scared to death. But if I'm being honest, I want the test to be positive. What about you?"

"I feel the exact same way." He leaned back without releasing her and gave her a dimpled smile. "I have a feeling it's going to be positive, and I also think we're going to have a boy."

Cree burst out laughing and swatted him away. "Of course you do, and I'm sure you've already decided what NFL team he'll play on. However, it might be a girl, and instead of us buying football gear, we'll be buying volleyballs and knee pads because we already know our kid is going to be tall."

For the next few minutes, they laughed and came up with one scenario after another on what it was going to be like to have a baby. Cree's nervousness from moments ago quickly turned into hope. She wanted the test to be positive, and she sent up a silent prayer.

"I guess we should go check," Tristan said.

When they returned to the bathroom, Cree was too nervous to look. So, Tristan did the honors. He stood there for a solid minute looking down at the white stick. When he looked up, his face was expressionless, until he broke out into a huge grin.

"Yes! We're having a baby!" He whooped and picked her up and started swinging her around but stopped abruptly.

"Shit, I shouldn't be doing that. You okay? How do you feel? Did I hurt you?"

He rattled off one anxious question after another, and Cree couldn't help but laugh. His excitement was contagious, and she was happier than she'd ever been.

"Oh my God, Cree... We're having a baby!"

***

If you enjoyed this story, please consider leaving a review on review sites or social media outlets.

Note from the author...

T hank you for reading SURRENDERING TO YOU! I hope you enjoyed Cree & Tristan as much as I enjoyed writing about them. Essence story is up next, and you'll get a chance to officially meet Jackson!

To the fans of my Atlanta's Finest series, did you catch that cameo of Dominic, Hamilton, and Dakota? Can you believe Dominic is in college now?! Who knows, maybe his Uncle Laz will pay him a visit at school during Essence's story. Stay tuned...

If you're new to my work, visit my website for a complete detailed list of my books.

***

Join Sharon's Mailing List

To get sneak peeks of upcoming stories and to hear about giveaways that Sharon is sponsoring,
click https://sharoncooper.net/newsletter to join her mailing list.

Other Titles By Sharon

Atlanta's Finest Series
Vindicated (book 1)
Indebted (book 2)
Accused (book 3)
Betrayed (book 4)
Hunted (book 5)
Tempted (book 6)
Committed (book 7)
Protected (book 7)

**Jenkins & Sons Construction Series
(Contemporary Romance)**
Love Under Contract (book 1)
Proposal for Love (book 2)
A Lesson on Love (book 3)
Unplanned Love (book 4)
Bid on Love (book 5)
The Cost of Love (book 6)

Jenkins Family Series (Contemporary Romance)
Best Woman for the Job (Short Story Prequel)
Still the Best Woman for the Job (book 1)
All You'll Ever Need (book 2)
Tempting the Artist (book 3)
Negotiating for Love (book 4)
Seducing the Boss Lady (book 5)
Love at Last (Holiday Novella)
When Love Calls (Novella)
More Than Love (Novella)

Reunited Series (Romantic Suspense)
Blue Roses (book 1)
Secret Rendezvous (Prequel to Rendezvous with Danger)
Rendezvous with Danger (book 2)
Truth or Consequences (book 3)
Operation Midnight (book 4)
Casino Heat (book 5)

Finding Love Series
Legal Seduction (Contemporary Romance)
A Dose of Passion (Contemporary Romance)
Model Attraction (Contemporary Romance)

Stand Alones
Something New ("Edgy" Sweet Romance)
Sin City Temptation (Contemporary Romance)
A Passionate Kiss (Contemporary Romance)
Soul's Desire (Unparalleled Love series)
Show Me (Irresistible Husband series)
His to Protect (Harlequin Romantic Suspense)

His to Defend (Harlequin Romantic Suspense)
Business Not As Usual (Romantic Comedy)
In It to Win It (Romantic Comedy)
Kiss Me (Irresistible Husband – Contemporary Romance)
Mr. One and Only (Baes of Juneteenth)
Fiancé for Hire (Men for Hire)

Priestly Family Series
Believing in You (Contemporary Romance)
Finding You (Contemporary Romance)
Daring to Love You (Contemporary Romance)
Surrendering to You (Contemporary Romance)

About the Author

USA Today bestselling author Sharon C. Cooper loves anything involving romance with a happily-ever-after, whether in books, movies, or real life. She writes contemporary romance, romantic suspense, as well as romantic comedy. She enjoys rainy days, carpet picnics, and family game night. Her stories have won numerous awards, including The Rochelle Alers Best Series award for her Atlanta's Finest Series (2022) and The Beverly Jenkins Author of the Year award (2021). When she isn't writing, Sharon loves hanging out with her amazing husband, doing volunteer work, or reading a good book (a romance of course). To read more about Sharon and her novels, or to sign up to be notified of her latest releases, visit www.sharoncooper.net

www.ingramcontent.com/pod-product-compliance
Lightning Source LLC
Chambersburg PA
CBHW050412260626
47156CB00003B/984